Jess recoiled from the map, pointing in amazement . . . Sure enough, the red cross was flickering about, drawn, erased and redrawn in different parts of the square. 'I thought we agreed treasure can't move?'

'It can if it's alive . . .' Jason pointed to the big cross. 'Don't you see, Jess? That's us.' Then he pointed to the smaller moving one. 'And that's Michael.' A shiver ran through him, and he swallowed hard. 'To whoever owns this map – *we're* the treasure!'

Also available:

Genie Us!
www.genieus.net

Series by Steve Cole
published by Red Fox:

Astrosaurs
Cows In Action
Astrosaurs Academy

Series by Linda Chapman
My Secret Unicorn
Not Quite a Mermaid
Stardust

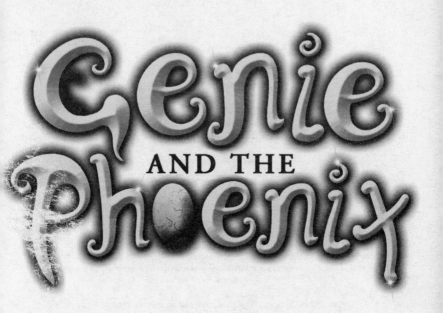

Genie

AND THE

Phoenix

STEVE COLE AND
LINDA CHAPMAN

www.kidsatrandomhouse.co.uk
www.rbooks.co.uk

ea es for inceptuces withn The Random House Group Lim
www.randomhouse.co.uk/offices.htm

THE RANDOM HOUSE GROUP Limited Reg. No

A CIP catalogue record for this book is available from the B

inted and bound in Great Britain by CPI Bookmarque, Cro

RED FOX

GENIE AND THE PHOENIX
A RED FOX BOOK 978 1 862 30384 3

First published in Great Britain by Red Fox,
an imprint of Random House Children's Books
A Random House Group Company

This edition published 2009

1 3 5 7 9 10 8 6 4 2

Set in Goudy Old Style

Red Fox Books are published by Random House Children's Books,
61–63 Uxbridge Road, London W5 5SA

www.kidsatrandomhouse.co.uk

Addr___ ___ ___ ___ Random House Group L___ted can be found at:
www.randomhouse.co.uk/offices.htm

THE RANDOM HOUSE ___ ___ ___ Limited Reg. ___ 954009

A CIP catalogue record for this ___ ___ available ___ British Library.

Pr___ted and bound in ___ ___ ___ ___ ___ ___ ___ydon, CR0 4TD

For our intrepid adventurers –
Spike, Amy, Tobey, Amany and Iola

With thanks to Sean O'Meara for being soccer supremo.

PROLOGUE

The room was eight-sided with high, dark walls. It was a place of magic.

A man stood gazing not through the windows in the walls, but at them. As if he could see patterns and images forming there in the glass. He approached the pane, his look hardening.

'The time draws near,' the man whispered, but no breath misted up the glass. 'The genie will find the bird of gold. A pact will be made. And four children with lives touched by magic shall brave death in the name of life . . .'

The man smiled and turned to the pale, shadowy figure behind him.

'Soon, my dear, the aching centuries will be behind us,' he promised. 'Power and majesty shall be ours once more. Creation will cringe at our feet and the stars will seem no more to us than sputtering candles, to let burn or snuff out as we choose.'

The figure held still in the shadows as the man stroked her cheek.

'The time of prophecy is at hand,' he murmured. 'The children are ready. Let their adventures begin anew. And let the fingers of fate tighten like a fist about them . . .'

Chapter One

Jason Worthington stood in the goal, his mouth dry, every muscle tensed. The ball flew towards him. His heart leaped. This was it. He was going to make the save! He launched himself to the side, arms outstretched . . .

The ball shot underneath him and slammed into the back of the net. He landed on the grass in a sprawling heap.

'Goal!' Milly's cry echoed around the park as she punched the air in triumph. She saw Jason's face and hastily let her arm drop. 'That was a really good try, Jase. You almost saved it!' She hurried over, offering a hand to help him up. 'I . . . I was just lucky.'

'And I was just rubbish!' Jason got up miserably. 'Even my eight-year-old stepsister can get a goal past me. No one ever wants me on their team, not even when they're just playing at break.'

Milly frowned. 'But if they're really your friends they should let you play. It shouldn't matter if you're good or not.'

'And back in the real world . . .' Jason rolled his eyes. Milly just didn't know what it was like to be left out. Whenever he saw her in the playground she always seemed to be surrounded by a gaggle of other girls, all chattering and wanting her to join in with their games. 'I wish I was better at sports.'

A faraway look stole into Milly's eyes. 'If Skribble was here he'd grant your wish . . .'

An image of a grumpy-looking worm glaring out of an old book flashed into Jason's mind. 'Milly,' he said awkwardly. 'Michael and Jess said that we shouldn't talk about genies and wishes and Skribble any more.'

Milly glanced across the park to where her thirteen-year-old brother Michael was slumped against an oak tree playing his Game Boy. Her stepsister, Jess, who was a year older than Michael, was standing near to him, talking to her best friend, Colette. 'Older brothers and sisters are a pain,' she said mutinously. 'Why do we have to do what they want all the time?'

A few months ago the four Worthingtons

had discovered an ancient book called *The Genie Handbook: Grant Wishes Like an Expert in Six Easy Stages* – a book full of *real* magic, complete with a fussy, grumpy, totally brilliant talking bookworm called Skribble. Together with Michael and Jess, Jason and Milly had used genie enchantments to grant actual wishes . . .

It had been the most incredible time of all their lives but they'd had to give up the magic in the end, and say goodbye to Skribble.

Jason looked at Milly. 'I think Jess and Michael were right – the more we all talk about the magical stuff, the harder it is to get used to normal life again.'

'But I don't *want* to get used to it!' Milly protested. 'They're just trying to be all boring and grown up.' She looked at Jason searchingly. 'You do still think about Skribble, don't you?'

'Sometimes.' Jason sighed. 'Look, there's no point talking about this – Skribble has gone and I can't get better at football by wishing. It's OK for you, Milly. You're good at loads of things – acting, singing, dancing . . .'

'I'm not *that* good,' Milly said, trailing after him. 'Nowhere near good enough to get the lead part in the big show.'

Jason looked at her in surprise. 'What do

you mean?' Ever since Milly had found out that her new after-school drama group was going to be doing a production of *Annie* she'd been going on and on about how she was sure she was going to be chosen to play the main part.

Milly sighed. 'We've been practising for the auditions this week.' She twisted her hands together and Jason noticed that for once her confidence seemed to have deserted her. 'And . . . well . . . some people in the group are really, really good at singing. Loads better than me.' She chewed her lip. 'I don't think I'm going to get to be Annie. But, oh, Jase, I really, really want to be!'

Jason frowned. Milly normally bounced around, thinking she could do anything and everything she wanted even without magic. 'I'm sure it'll be OK.'

'I'm sure it won't,' said Milly.

Feeling awkward, Jason changed the subject. 'Come on. I suppose I should do some more practising before we have to go home.'

Practice was on his older sister's mind too – essay practice. *I haven't done any*, Jess thought gloomily, leaning back against the oak. *It's just too hard. And I bet Colette has done loads this half term . . .*

'Jess, you look miles away,' said Colette with

a smile. 'Can you come into town with me then? We should make the most of the holiday before school starts again.'

Jess looked tempted but shook her head. 'I'd love to but I really should revise.' She pushed a hand through her straight blonde hair. 'Oh, Colette. I can't believe our exams are only just over a week away.'

'You'll be OK,' Colette reassured her.

'I won't. I am *so* going to fail history. I can never remember anything. And if I do fail then I won't be able to take it next year with you and Natasha and Jodie.' Jess shook her head in frustration. 'I really had better get back.' She waved impatiently at Milly and Jason, who were playing football again, beckoning them over. 'Revision's no worse than babysitting, I guess.'

'Well, OK,' Colette said sympathetically. 'Good luck with it. See you at school on Monday.' She set off but then stopped. 'Oh, Michael,' she said, as if noticing him for the first time. 'You're friends with that new boy, aren't you? I've seen you hanging round with him.'

Michael frowned. 'Who, Rick? *He* hangs round with *me!*'

'Whatever. If you see him, tell him I said hi.'

Colette grinned quickly at Jess. 'Laters!' she said and headed into town.

Michael buried his head in his hands. 'Good ole Rick the Slick,' he said bitterly, glancing up through his fingers at Jess. 'Even the girls in your year fancy him! It's not natural. It's not fair.'

'Well, he is quite fit,' Jess reasoned. 'And he's really tall. You'd never have known he was just a Year Eight.'

'Yeah, yeah. Oh, and he just happens to have loads of cash, amazing rugby skills and a dad who acts on the telly.' Michael shook his head, making his dark fringe flop into his eyes. 'How can people be taken in by that stuff?'

'I wonder,' Jess said dryly. She frowned. 'Anyway, if you don't like him, how come you're always hanging out together at school.'

'Not my choice,' Michael shot back. 'As soon as he started at school, I knew he'd be trouble, but all my so-called mates think he's great. It's really bugging me. Wherever I look he's always there.'

'Count yourself lucky if that's your only problem,' Jess sighed. 'OK, so it's annoying that this cool kid has come along and all your mates think he's amazing, but at least you haven't got mega-important exams coming up. I won't even *be* with my friends if I fail—'

'Uh-huh. I know,' muttered Michael. 'Life sucks.'

Jess nodded in agreement.

Just then Milly and Jason reached them. 'Hi, guys,' said Jason. 'Is everything OK?'

Michael snorted.

'Everything's fine,' said Jess despondently. 'But I need to revise some more, so we'd better go home now.'

'Home. Huh!' Michael got to his feet. 'A boring old house in boring old Moreways Meet, at least a gazillion miles from anywhere remotely cool. Why can't anything exciting ever happen round here? It's just boring, boring, boring!'

Suddenly a large piece of yellowing paper blew across the grass and wrapped around Jess's legs. 'Ew!' she said, reaching down to pull it away. As she did so, Jason saw that it had a drawing and words on it.

'Hang on!' He stopped Jess before she could crumple it up. 'It looks like a map or something. Maybe someone's lost it.'

Jess straightened out the paper. Michael had already lost interest and flicked open his Game Boy again, but Milly nudged up to Jason and took a look. Jason immediately saw that he'd been right. It *was* a map, and a very old one by the look of it. The paper was thick, yellowed with age, with rips and tears around the edges. There were lots of roads or paths marked out in dark lines, six of which crossed in the middle of the map. There were a few funny zigzags and lots of wonky rectangles, some of which were surrounded by drawings of bushes or trees. A tall thin tangle of squares sat in the top right corner of the map, like the artist had drawn several shapes on top of each other. There was some old-fashioned writing at the top, scrawled in a scratchy ink pen, but Jason couldn't make out the words. His attention was taken more by a thick red cross marked beside one of the trees.

Jess looked about. She saw a couple of mums with buggies and some pensioners playing bowls, but no one looked as though they'd lost something. Then she glanced back at the map. 'It looks a bit like Moreways Meet,' she said. 'Six roads that meet in the middle, just like in the town centre near Mum and Mark's shop.'

'The whole reason we had to move to this dump,' Michael muttered. 'Just so they could live their dream of opening a mouldy old book shop!'

Milly suddenly squealed like a guinea pig with a megaphone. Jess jumped and Michael almost dropped his Game Boy. 'LOOK! It's . . . It's a . . .' Milly could hardly get her words out she was so excited. She stabbed her finger at the scrawled words on the top of the map. 'It's a *treasure map.*'

They all stared at her. Michael got up and joined the others in staring at the map.

Jess frowned at the words at the top of the parchment. 'A *Map for Those Who Seek Hidden Treasures*,' she read out slowly.

'I couldn't read that a moment ago!' Jason whispered. 'It was just a scrawl. Honest!'

'Oh, wow!' Milly exclaimed. 'A *magic* treasure map! I told you exciting stuff could happen!'

'Milly, stop!' said Jess swiftly. 'Jason can't have looked properly, that's all.'

'Exactly,' Michael sneered. 'I mean, a magic treasure map? How likely is that?'

Milly put her hands on her hips. 'How likely is it that we found a talking bookworm in a book telling us how to be genies?'

'Milly!' Jess sighed. 'You know we agreed not to talk about that.'

'You mean, *you* agreed we wouldn't talk about it,' Milly retorted, her eyes shining with excitement. 'It is a magic map. I bet it is! I bet that now magic's happened to us once, it's going to keep on happening!'

Jason's eyes were glued to the map. 'I think maybe you're right,' he said breathlessly.

Michael groaned. 'Yeah, yeah, eight-year-old expert Milly is right – oh, and there goes a pig flying out of my butt!'

'No, look!' Holding the map out to Michael, Milly and Jess in one trembling hand, Jason pointed at the bottom of the map where seven words were written: *Know Yourself, Trust Yourself, Believe in Yourself.*

Seven words that *hadn't* been there when they had first opened up the map!

Jess paled. 'You're right, Jase,' she whispered. 'Those words really have just appeared. It *must* be magic!'

'Give it here.' Michael took the map gingerly from Jason and looked at it from all angles. 'If this is a wind-up . . .'

'It's not!' Milly hugged Jason and Jess. 'It's magic and it's real! You saw it yourself, Michael, you *can't* say you don't believe now!'

There was a long pause while everyone looked at Michael. Slowly a grin spread across his face. 'Who's not believing? Have you met my flying butt-pig?' He clapped his Game Boy shut with one hand and waved the map in the air with the other. 'Oink! Oink! Look out, treasure – here we come!'

Chapter Two

Milly jumped up and down in delight and Michael shoved the others out of the way to spread out the map on the grass. 'OK, let's see what we've got here . . .'

The others crowded round. 'This must be where the treasure is!' Michael banged his finger down on the red cross. 'Now, whereabouts do we start? We need some landmarks or something.'

'But we don't even know it's definitely Moreways Meet,' said Jess. 'I know that crossroads is like the one in the centre of town, but look at the rest of the map . . .'

Jason saw what she meant, and his excitement ebbed a little. 'One tree on a map usually means lots of trees in real life,' he remarked. 'It looks like these roads are in a forest or something. There aren't any buildings marked on either.'

'What about these things?' Michael pointed to a square near to the crossroads and then the strange, multi-layered squares. 'They could be buildings.'

Milly peered closely at the paper. 'Look! I thought these were just ink marks dotted about, but now they look more like tiny words.'

'Let me see.' Jason peered at one piece of microscopic scrawl beside a forest path. 'A . . . S . . . H,' he spelled out. 'Ash.'

Milly shrugged. 'Maybe it means there's a pile of ash we have to look for.'

'This one says beech,' said Jess, squinting at another.

Michael pulled a face. 'There aren't any beaches anywhere near here.'

'Beech as in beech tree,' said Jess.

'And an ash is a kind of tree,' Jason realized.

Michael's eyes lit up. 'It's a code we have to crack! Yeah, that'll be it!'

Jess nodded. 'Let's go home and write down all the words properly and try to work out what the map is showing us.'

'Smart one,' said Michael. 'Come on then!'

Jason hesitated. 'I was just thinking . . . Where did the map come from?' The others all looked at him. 'I mean, a map like this must be really valuable. It's old – and it's magic. Why was it just blowing around a park?'

'Who cares where it came from?' said Michael. 'Finders keepers!'

'I dunno.' Jess bit her lip. 'Maybe we *should* leave it here for its owner to find.'

'No way! Look, think about it like this,' reasoned Michael. 'It just appeared, didn't it? Maybe we're meant to have it 'cause we've done magic before – like Milly said. Come on, guys, this is a magic treasure map! We can't just chuck it away.'

'Michael's right,' said Milly. 'We can't!'

Jason looked anxiously at his sister. He felt they probably should try and find who'd lost it but he really, really didn't want to. He wanted to go hunting for treasure!

Jess did a strange half-nod, half-shake of her head. 'Oh, all right. Let's take it home.'

Jason felt a rush of relief. 'Brilliant!'

He and the others hurried away in an excited huddle, treasuring their secret, all their boring worries forgotten. And so they never noticed a mysterious rustling noise coming from a nearby bush, nor the curl of golden smoke that rose up from within it . . .

No sooner had Jess turned the key in the front door lock than Michael had pushed past her, waving the map like a flag. 'Gangway!' he yelled, charging towards their den in the basement. It was part junk room, part cellar, with an old sofa, piles of boxes and wonky chairs. They cleared a space on the floor and laid out the map, holding down the corners with a random assortment of objects – a chipped china ornament of a little girl, a glass vase, an old casserole dish and a purple paperweight. Their parents were out, working in their busy book shop.

'Now, let's have a proper look at this thing,' said Michael.

'But . . . but . . .' Jess felt a shiver run through her and her mouth went dry. She pointed at the red cross on the map. 'The cross has moved!'

They all stared. The cross was no longer beside the tree. It was now in the strange tangle of squares in the top right corner.

'But how can it have *moved*?' Milly said. 'Treasure can't move!'

'Weird,' breathed Michael.

Jason looked at the red cross. Some of the scratchy ink lines seemed to be drawn over it, like it had been placed at the bottom of the layers. He moved his head from side to side, looking at the shapes within the shapes. There was something really familiar about them all. From the position

17

of the six-way crossroads, the layered shapes weren't a million miles from their house, but he couldn't think of any landmark nearby that would match that design.

'I wonder . . .' Jason traced the ink lines with his finger. They looked like partitions . . . or walls . . . was this a staircase . . . ?

'Hey, Jase, go and find a magnifying glass,' said Michael. 'Let's see if we can read any more of the words and get some clues to what's going on.'

Jess frowned at Michael. 'Who made Jason your slave? You get the magnifying glass.'

Michael gave a long-suffering sigh and loped away up the stairs. The door to the den slammed shut behind him.

And Jason, still watching the map, suddenly stiffened. 'No way,' he breathed.

Jess had turned to Milly. 'I wonder what the treasure is?'

'Gold and jewels!' said Milly immediately.

Jason gulped. 'I don't think so. Look!'

Jess and Milly turned. Jason was pointing wordlessly at the tangle of overlaid squares, his eyes wide and fearful. Milly gasped.

There wasn't just one cross now. There were two!

One cross still sat in the lower layer of the overlapping shapes, while a smaller cross had appeared on top of the scratchy black lines.

'What . . . what's happening?' Jess asked, intrigued. 'What does it mean?'

'I think that those squares and shapes represent our house,' Jason began, 'viewed from above as if it's all see-through.'

Milly stared at him. 'You mean all the different floors are . . . sort of on top of each other?'

'Right. I knew I recognized it!' Jason started to talk rapidly, pointing at the different layers. 'See, this must be the den where we are.' He ran his finger along the dotted lines. 'That's the staircase. And then up above that is the kitchen and the hall and the lounge – the dotted lines are the walls. And the next square up is divided into the bedrooms, with Michael's right at the top.'

'So some of the treasure is in our house!' Milly cried. 'Cool! But, hang on . . . why are there two crosses?'

Jess recoiled from the map, pointing in amazement. 'And why is one moving?' Sure enough, the red cross was flickering about, drawn, erased and redrawn in different parts of the square. 'I thought we agreed treasure can't move?'

'It can if it's alive . . .' Jason pointed to the

big cross. 'Don't you see, Jess? That's us.' Then he pointed to the smaller moving one. 'And that's Michael.' A shiver ran through him, and he swallowed hard. 'To whoever owns this map – *we're* the treasure!'

Chapter Three

Jess, Jason and Milly watched the little red cross blink in and out of existence on the old yellowed paper. And although they were expecting the den door to rattle open as Michael entered, they all still jumped.

'What's got you lot so spooked?' Michael said.

Ten seconds and one stammered explanation later, he had his answer.

'*We're* the treasure?' he spluttered. 'But that's crazy!'

'Look at the whole map.' Jason's freckled face was pale. 'This wonky rectangle must be the park and the bigger ones at the bottom are most likely our school buildings. The smaller box by the crossroads has to be Mum and Mark's shop.'

'It's a map of all the places we're most likely to be found together,' said Milly.

Jess got up from the floor. 'Watch what happens when I go out of the room.'

She left the basement. Michael saw a small red cross move up from the lower layer into the next layer.

'See?' Milly whispered.

'I do see.' Michael gulped. 'And I don't like.'

Jess came back downstairs, her face creased with worry. 'The cross moved, didn't it? Whoever this map belonged to is trying to find us!'

Just then there was a knock on the door. All four of them jumped about a mile in the air. 'Hi! Is anyone home?'

'It's Mum!' hissed Jason. 'Quick! Hide the map.'

'Hi, Mum!' Jess called as Milly rolled it up. 'We're just . . . um, down here!'

There was the sound of footsteps on the stairs and, just as Milly shoved the map under the sofa, Ann Worthington looked over the banister. 'What on earth are you all doing down here when it's such a lovely afternoon?'

'Just hanging out,' said Jess.

'Kicking back,' Michael agreed.

'How was the shop?' Milly asked, a fixed smile on her face.

'Good,' said Ann. 'I was just going to do some baked potatoes for supper. Can someone give them a scrub for me?'

'I will,' said Jason, getting to his feet. The thought of being close to grown-ups and doing something ordinary and dull seemed suddenly *very* comforting. The others must have thought so too as they quickly followed him.

Mark Worthington, Michael and Milly's dad, was in the kitchen setting the table. 'Here comes the posse,' he said brightly. 'All right, everyone?'

They all smiled briefly but no one said anything.

'You're quiet,' Mark commented. 'Has it been a tough day then? I wish parents got half-term holidays. I'd love a week just hanging about with nothing much to do.'

'Yeah, me too,' Ann sighed. 'I could go shopping, see my friends, do some more pottery . . . talking of which, Jess, I know you've got lots of studying to do, but do you think you could pop round to Mr Milton's workshop with Milly? He came in to the shop today to say he's fired those pots we made.'

'I guess,' Jess said reluctantly. One of the customers at the shop had an old workshop with a kiln and when he'd found out Ann dabbled in pottery he'd insisted she used the kiln whenever she wanted. Ann had taken Milly there the other day and they'd made some wonky pots together.

'I'm glad you're sending the girls along in your place, Ann,' said Mark with a mischievous smile.

'I still say Mr Milton fancies you!'

'He does not!' Ann protested. 'He's just a lonely old man trying to be friendly. You should see his house, it's enormous! And the grounds are full of the most amazing sculptures.'

'Sounds awesome,' said Michael wryly.

Ann ignored his sarcasm. 'We'll have to find time to go and glaze those pots, Milly.'

'Maybe after my audition,' Milly agreed.

'Ah, yes,' said her dad with a smile. 'You'll soon be swapping the art studio for a recording studio!'

'Can I go and practise my singing now, Dad?' asked Milly.

'And I was thinking I should do some revision,' said Jess quickly.

'Good girl,' said Ann approvingly. 'Milly, perhaps you should sing in the shed if Jess is trying to work.'

'Outside? On my own?' Milly froze. Michael gave her a warning look, and she sighed. 'It's a bit spidery out there. Maybe I'll just practise quietly in the lounge.'

She hurried from the room.

'So it's OK for me to play on my Game Boy,' said Michael. 'Right?'

'Wrong,' said Mark flatly. 'Revision and singing practice get you out of setting the table, playing your Game Boy doesn't. Cutlery, please.'

Michael rolled his eyes and stomped over to the cutlery drawer.

Jason began washing the potatoes. He couldn't stop thinking about the map. Who was looking for them? What were the tree names supposed to mean? Jason didn't like puzzles without answers.

Then again, he thought with a shiver, if someone scary was trying to find them, he might not like the answers even more.

Later that evening, after eating her supper without tasting it, Jess stared miserably at the history books laid out neatly on her desk. Milly was just getting into bed, fidgeting from side to side. Usually, Jess moved out to the study when Milly wanted to sleep but now she looked over at her stepsister huddling down under the duvet.

'Hey,' Jess said softly. 'Are you OK?'

'I think so.' Milly swallowed. 'I mean, if someone nasty was looking for us, they can't find us now, can they? We've got the map.'

'Right,' Jess agreed.

'But –' Milly's eyes widened in alarm at the thought – 'what if they threw the map away because they don't need it any more – because they've already found us!'

Jess felt as if an ice cube had just scraped down her spine. 'Oh, Milly, you and your imagination!'

she said quickly. 'Now, I really must do some revision . . .' She looked back at the open book on her desk. She'd read the same paragraph sixteen times, and still all she could see was little red crosses scuttling across the page.

Magic, she thought anxiously. *We're better off without it!*

The next morning, Jason lay in bed, waiting until he heard his mum and Mark leave for the shop. He hadn't felt like going downstairs and chatting to them as he normally did. He felt exhausted. In his dreams he'd been running from some unknown menace through a dark forest full of strange trees.

Pushing back the covers, he got out of bed and padded downstairs. The house was still and quiet.

Jason jumped as Milly came into the kitchen.

'Sorry,' she said quickly. 'I didn't mean to startle you.'

''S OK,' said Jason. 'It's just . . . I keep thinking about the map . . .'

'So do I,' said Jess, yawning as she came in. 'Hi, you two. Did you sleep all right?'

'No,' said Jason. 'The map is still freaking me out.'

'And me,' Milly added.

Jess sighed. 'Me too. Let's get Michael up and start talking about it.'

'Michael *is* up.' Michael shambled into the kitchen in his boxer shorts and T-shirt, waving the map. 'I wondered where you'd all gone, then I saw the red crosses on this thing . . .'

Milly shivered. 'Don't, Michael.'

'Look,' said Jess sharply. 'Just because this magic treasure map has turned up, it doesn't automatically mean we're going to be up to our necks in crazy, freaky stuff all over again—'

'Hey,' Jason interrupted. 'Can anyone smell something strange?'

Michael sniffed the air. 'Yeah. I just assumed it was Jess.'

'Shut up!' Jess said witheringly. She twitched her nose. 'Actually, I *can* smell something. It smells like smoke.'

They glanced around the kitchen but nothing was burning. Milly got up and looked out of the window. She gasped. 'The shed! The shed's on fire!'

The others ran to the window. Sure enough, the small, poky shed in the garden full of Mark's rusting tools was wreathed in smoke.

'Oh no!' Jess's hand flew to her mouth. 'We'd better call the fire brigade! Where's the phone?' She started to search the cluttered worktops.

Michael joined in, hastily sweeping piles of papers and bills on to the floor. 'It must be around here somewhere.'

'Something just moved in the shed!' cried Jason.

'I saw it too!' Milly gasped. 'Something moved past the window.'

Jess stared. 'What? You mean, there's someone in there?'

'I'll check it out,' cried Michael, throwing open the back door. 'If it gets around school that I'm a hero who saved someone's life, I'll definitely be one up on Rick the Slick! Come on, Jase.'

'Don't you dare get too close,' Jess warned them. 'Oh, where *is* the phone?'

'I think one of them is in our bedroom. I'll go and get it!' Milly fled from the kitchen.

'Get my mobile if you can't find it,' shouted Jess. 'It's on the bedside table!'

Heart racing, Michael bundled Jason through the door ahead of him, steering him out into the garden and towards the shed. The smoke was wafting across the lawn, and Michael coughed as he breathed in a mouthful. It was strangely fragrant and made his head tingle.

Jason went rigid, and pointed his finger. 'There it is again – movement. There's definitely someone in there!'

'Or some*thing*. Probably a sparrow or something.' Michael peered through the haze. 'OK, I'm going in. You wait here, Jase. I just hope I'm not risking my neck to help some stupid bird!'

Covering his mouth with his arm, he headed for the shed door. Thick smoky tendrils were curling out from under it. Michael grabbed the handle of the door with his free hand and pulled.

A cloud of smoke exploded towards him. He reeled back with a yell.

'What a to-do!' came a loud, female voice from inside as he fell onto the grass, speechless with shock. 'I set your little house on fire – that's not good manners! Ooooh, I *am* sorry. But thank you so much for getting me out . . .'

So, there *was* a person in the shed! Michael wiped his stinging eyes. 'Who's there?' he shouted, starting to get up and peering through the smoke. 'Are you all right?'

'Me, dearie? Oh yes, I'm fine!' There was a flash of gold in the smoke. 'You two look a bit peaky though.'

Michael and Jason stared, dumbstruck in amazement, as a bizarre golden bird about the size of a turkey came waddling out of the shed towards them. She cocked her head on one side and her beak seemed to curve into a smile. 'Hello, loveys!'

'It's a bird!' burbled Jason, pointing wildly. 'Michael, it's . . . it's a talking bird!'

'Jess! Milly!' Michael called in a high-pitched, frightened screech as he fell back down on his bottom. 'Get out here! NOW!'

Chapter Four

The golden bird blinked. 'Goodness what a noise!' she cried. 'I'm sorry to give you such a turn, but don't fret, pet. It wasn't much of a fire.' She fluffed up her incredible golden feathers. 'Anyway, thank you so much for letting me out of there. This beak of mine is no good for opening doors and the smoke was getting rather thick, so I really am ever so grateful for your bravery.' She gave Michael a fond look. 'Now, what was that you were saying earlier about risking your neck to help a bird, young man? Because, oh! does *this* bird ever need some help!'

Michael stared. With her spiky feathers and sharply curving beak, the bird looked to have been sculpted from real gold. Her face was oddly expressive – proud but friendly with glittering sapphire eyes and long eyelashes. The air seemed to ripple around her like a heat haze, though the shed had stopped burning.

The bird waddled a bit closer to Michael. 'Speak up, lovey – who are you, what's your name? Come on, don't be shy!'

Michael backed away on his bottom as if from a rattlesnake. 'I'm dreaming!'

'"Dreaming", you say?' The bird looked crestfallen. 'Well, young Master Dreaming, I must have the wrong place again. I'm so sorry to have bothered you. I had hoped that the Worthington children lived here . . .'

'They do!' Jason blinked. 'I mean, *we* do.'

Michael whacked him on the arm. 'Don't tell it stuff!'

'*You* are the Worthingtons?' The bird flew up excitedly into the air. 'Oh, the Fire Mountain be praised! Then I *have* found you at last!'

'Found us?' Jason asked in wonder. 'You mean, the map—'

Michael whacked his arm again. 'Shut up, Jase!'

'Jase as in Jason!' The bird flapped in a circle. 'Oh, my little treasures!' she trilled. 'I've been looking for you everywhere, and now I've found you!'

Michael heard footsteps on the lawn behind him and turned to see Jess and Milly racing towards them. They saw the golden bird dancing in the air and skidded to an incredulous halt.

'Oh . . . *wow!*' breathed Milly.

'Four of you!' cooed the bird rapturously. 'Just as he said there would be. Four Worthingtons here in front of my very eyes: Master Jason, Master Michael, Mistress Milly and Mistress Jess! Am I right? Please, tell me I'm right.'

Jason opened his mouth to speak then looked at Michael warily.

'Yes, you're completely right!' said Milly, her eyes shining in wonder.

Michael groaned. 'You're as bad as Jase!'

But his sister ignored him totally. 'Who are you, bird? *What* are you?'

'I think I know,' Jason said quickly. 'You're a *phoenix*, aren't you?'

The bird gave a delighted screech. 'Ooooh! I can see Skribble was spot on about you. Sharp as a new pin he said you were. Yes, you're dead right. I am a phoenix – *the* phoenix to be precise. There's only me. I'm the only phoenix in the whole wide world!' She looked round at them all. 'My name's Fenella. Pleased to meet you.'

'Fenella the Phoenix?' Jess echoed. Michael groaned weakly again.

'Wait a moment . . .' Still in shock, it had taken a few seconds for Milly to process what the bird had said. '*Skribble* was spot on? Do you mean to say you know Skribble?'

'Me? Know Skribbaleum El Lazeez Ekir?' Fenella chuckled. 'Oh yes, my little chickabiddy!

And what a worm he is!' She affected a swoon. 'Ooooh, if I were seven hundred years younger . . . So clever he is! If I hadn't lost that wonderful magic map he gave me I'd have found you a lot sooner. I remembered the general area but when you reach my age, you get a little hazy about the details . . .'

'Magic map?' Jess said wonderingly.

'It was leading you to us!' Milly realized.

'And that's why the names of the trees were marked on!' Jason finally cracked the puzzle. 'You were navigating by them as you flew overhead . . .'

'We wanted magic back in our lives,' Milly whispered, her eyes shining as she stared at Fenella. 'And now we've got it!'

Jess nodded dubiously. 'But if there's one thing Skribble taught us, it's be careful what you wish for.'

'You must be Jess,' said Fenella. 'Skribble said you were the sensible one.' She looked at Milly and her smile grew wider. 'And this pretty little chicken is young Milly, I presume. I can see why Skribble has a soft spot for you! Kind and sweet and fair, he told me!'

Milly glowed with pleasure.

'And Jason, the bright boy who saw me for what I am. "Perceptive." That's how Skribble described you!' Finally Fenella's blue eyes fixed on

Michael with a look of surprise. 'And so you must be Michael. I must say, I can't see what Skribble was talking about.'

Michael's eyes narrowed. '*What* did the worm say?'

'Oh don't worry about that, pet,' Fenella said hastily. 'He can't have meant it. Just his idea of a little joke, I'm sure. You seem a very fine, upstanding young man to me.' She looked at him from under her eyelashes. 'And so brave, trying to rescue me like that! Oooh, such chivalry makes my feathers tingle.'

Michael blushed and Milly giggled.

'So, why are you here?' Jess asked. 'Why did Skribble tell you to find us?'

With a cheerful laugh, Fenella hopped down from the shed and looked at them hopefully. 'I have a little favour to ask you. Skribble said he was sure you would help. However, I'm feeling a bit chilly right now.' Fenella shivered and then looked towards the shed. 'Do you think we could maybe pop inside your little home and discuss it?'

'That's not where we live,' Milly said, realizing the bird thought they lived in the shed. 'It's where Dad keeps his tools.'

'Is it?' Fenella struck her forehead with her wing. 'Dearie me, aren't I silly? Skribble said you lived in a den, you see.'

'Our den is a room inside that big house,' said Milly, pointing behind her. 'Would you like to go there?'

'Yes, please, pet,' said Fenella. 'I've cooled off my feathers now so I won't start any more blazes—'

'Hang on, hang on,' Michael interrupted. 'What is this favour the worm said we'd help you with?'

Fenella gave Michael a coy look. 'Cut to the chase, eh? Very well then, I'll go and get my reason for coming here! Back in a mo. Don't go away.' She flapped back inside the shed.

'Wow!' breathed Milly. 'Isn't she wonderful?'

Jess grinned at Michael. 'She seems to like *you*, her brave young man.'

Crossing his arms and hunching his shoulders, Michael glared at his stepsister. 'I'm just glad it was no one bad after us.'

'I wonder what she's gone to get,' said Jason.

Just then Fenella emerged with what looked to be a smooth, red-gold rugby ball under one wing.

'What's that?' asked Milly in astonishment.

'Strange and baffling is what it is, my little jam puddings.' Fenella plonked the gleaming object on the grass. 'I've laid an egg! Me, the one and only phoenix!' She looked both proud and puzzled. 'I mean, what's *that* all about?'

Jess, Milly and Michael exchanged confused

looks. 'Um . . . what's so weird about a bird laying an egg?' said Michael.

But Jason was nodding excitedly as if he understood. 'The phoenix doesn't need an egg. There's just her. She lives to be really old and then sort of bursts into flame and is reborn from her ashes. You come back, don't you, Fenella – time and time again . . .'

'That's it exactly, lovey,' said Fenella proudly. 'I go up in smoke, my ashes sit around for a while, then they catch light and I'm reborn as a brand new, bright-eyed and ever so slightly *slinky* phoenix! Well, a girl can dream!' She threw back her beak and laughed raucously. 'There was this one time I came back with the biggest, featheriest bottom you ever saw. Every time I flew up to my nest, it was like an eclipse of the sun!'

She gave another noisy peal of laughter, but Milly looked alarmed. 'Poor Fenella, burning up like that . . . doesn't it hurt?'

'No, lovey, not a bit!' Fenella reassured her. 'The whole magnificent process tickles more than anything. I do like a bit of heat . . .' She shivered, and looked hopefully at the children.

'Let's go inside,' urged Jess. 'You can tell us more when we're in the den.'

'Ooooh, thank you.' Fenella looked delighted. 'Just lead the way!'

A few minutes later, Fenella was perched on a

big squashy beanbag in the middle of the den, her egg tucked between her feet and her tummy, her plumage softly glittering in the sunlight streaming through the window. The children sat in front of her, Jason and Milly on the floor, Michael and Jess on the sofa.

'Can I stroke you?' Milly asked, looking at the phoenix in awe.

The bird beamed. 'Oh, yes. I do like a bit of stroking now and then. And I've lowered my temperature, so you'll be quite safe.'

Milly tentatively stroked Fenella's golden back. It was like stroking a feathery hot-water bottle. 'Is that OK?'

Fenella cooed and rearranged her wings. 'That's lovely. I am sorry about your workbench in the shed, you know.'

'Don't worry. Mark hardly ever goes in there,' said Jess. 'He won't notice for ages.'

Fenella sighed. 'I'm usually quite good at keeping my cool but I'm getting these hot flushes at the moment. It'll be my age. I've burned up and come back at least twenty times, you know. Once every thousand years . . .'

'That's well ancient!' Michael said in awe.

'I prefer to use the word "mature",' said Fenella.

'That's not a word in Michael's vocabulary,' Jess assured her.

Keen to solve the mystery, Jason leaned eagerly towards the golden bird. 'So, if you normally come back out of ashes, why have you laid an egg?'

'That's what I'd like to know, sweet pea!' the phoenix said. 'I've only laid an egg once before – about five centuries ago. I woke up one morning with a bit of a dicky tummy and then, *pop*! Out it came!'

'But then . . .' Jason frowned. 'Does this mean you *aren't* the only phoenix in the world?'

'No, no. There's still just me. You see . . . the egg didn't hatch. I went and lost it.' Fenella's smile slipped a little. 'Typical me. I laid it – then I *mis*laid it soon after. Oooh, I was ever so upset.' One of her blue eyes brimmed with a golden tear, which fell with a smoky sizzle onto her plumage. 'It gets lonely, you see, being the one and only phoenix. It would be my wish come true to have someone to look after. Someone I could share the years with. But alas, there it was – my one shot at bringing a new little phoenix into the world, or so I thought, and I'd blown it.' Her golden brow creased with determination. 'But now I've been given a second chance and I'll not mess things up again. I'll hatch this egg whatever it takes.' She twittered. 'Unfortunately, it seems to take *a lot*. At least, so Skribbaleum says, and he is an expert.'

Jess raised an eyebrow. 'He is?'

Milly clasped her hands together. 'How *is* Skribble? Is he OK? Did somebody nice pick up the lamp we put him in? Did they—'

'So many questions, my little duckling!' Fenella chuckled. 'I'm not entirely sure what's happened to him since he bade you *au revoir*, but I bumped into him in Morocco.'

'Morocco?' Jason echoed. 'Wow! What was he doing there?'

'Well,' said Fenella, rustling her feathers with the air of someone who has a story to tell. 'Just picture it. There I was, perched in a tree in the Souss Massa National Park one beautiful summer's evening, just a few weeks back, when I heard these angry voices overhead. It was two humans in a hot-air balloon! Rough fellers they were – proper hooligans – fighting over a magic lamp!' She shook her head disapprovingly. 'They tussled and the lamp fell out of the basket. Just like that! It came tumbling past my beak and ended up on the forest floor.' Fenella smiled. 'I picked it up, rubbed the side and out popped Skribble.'

Jess was full of excitement. 'So what did he *say?*'

'Well, I took him back to my nest for a lovely cup of green tea and it turned out he knew a prophecy about my egg! He'd read it while locked up in the Great Genie Library all that time ago.' Fenella cooed proudly. 'Just think, me and my little egg in a prophecy in the Genie Library! How grand is that?'

'What did the prophecy say?' Michael asked.

Fenella ruffled her feathers proudly. 'That any egg I lay contains "power unheard of in all the realms" and that if it is to hatch properly I have to build a very special nest and get hold of four extra-rare ingredients.'

'What are they?' asked Jason eagerly.

Fenella's voice grew grander, more theatrical. 'To hatch a phoenix egg, one needs four wondrous things. First, a . . .' She paused and then looked crestfallen. 'Actually, loveys, I've forgotten. Have you got my map there?'

'Hold on . . .' Jason pulled it out of his back pocket – and gasped. 'It's changed!' he squeaked. 'The map doesn't show our house and Moreways Meet any more.'

'Of course not,' chuckled Fenella as Michael, Milly and Jess crowded round to see. 'It's a magic map, remember? And since I've found you, it doesn't need to lead me here any longer – so it's showing what I've got to find next. Remind me, Michael, pet, would you?'

Michael stared. The yellowed paper now displayed four intricate line drawings – one depicting the sun with a strange pattern scratched all over it; one showing an old Egyptian pyramid topped with a bundle of sticks; one illustrating a mountain peak covered by a leaf-shaped rain cloud; and the final image describing a kind of deformed stick of celery with leaves like hands and a heart perched on top. A few lines of exotic, slanted handwriting accompanied each of the cryptic scenes.

He read aloud:

'If the hatching of a Phoenix Egg is to be properly achieved . . .

'One: You must capture a shaft of tomorrow's sunshine and spin that glorious light into golden thread; said thread to be thrice-woven between the sticks and fibres of the birthing nest to ensure the hatchling's fine fortune.

'Two: You must acquire the ashes of the last phoenix nest from old Cairo, which when scattered in the new nest shall impart wisdom and experience to the hatchling.

'Three: You must harvest a stalk of silphium, that fine rare herb which can be found deep in the rainforests of Peru. Polish the eggshell with said stalk to aid balance, grace and precision of movement in the hatchling.

'Four: You must gather the first dewdrop from the summit of the sacred Mount of Quamquangle at the Hour of Sun-Arise, and daub the drop upon the eggshell so as to ensure the hatchling sings in tones the sweetest.'

Michael put down the map and sighed. 'Something tells me this is going to take more than a quick trip to Tesco.'

Fenella nodded wisely. 'It will take magic, ingenuity and a good deal of courage.'

'So, is this why Skribble told you to find us, Fenella?' asked Milly excitedly. 'He wants us to help you get all these things?'

Fenella nodded. 'I'm a little bit on the forgetful side, as you might have noticed, and me and maps, well – we just don't get along. I don't stand a chance of gathering all those things, not with time pressing the way it is.'

'And so Skribble said we'd help,' said Jason.

Michael nodded glumly. 'Cheers, Worm.'

'Of course we'll help,' Milly exclaimed.

Fenella preened herself. 'Well, if you do, you won't find me ungenerous. I'll pay you – in gold.'

Michael gasped. 'Gold?'

'Special phoenix gold.' Fenella nodded proudly. 'Magical stuff, spun from the sunlight.'

'Is it worth something though,' Michael pressed her eagerly, 'like real gold?'

'It puts real gold in the shade!' the phoenix exclaimed. 'I've seen men fight to the death for a speck of the stuff in the markets of old Cairo. Rarer than an eagle's tears and brighter than the Pole Star, it is.'

'Gold . . .' Michael's eyes were agleam. 'I can see it now – move over Rick the Slick, there's a new millionaire in town!'

'Shut up a minute, Michael.' Jess looked searchingly at the golden bird. 'Fenella, you said something about time pressing. What did you mean by that?'

Fenella sighed. Her body seemed to deflate a little. 'I'm nearing the end of my life, dearies. In this old body, anyway.'

Milly frowned. 'What?'

'I've come to know the signs, you see,' the phoenix went on. 'Feeling the cold, losing my way, overheating. In a matter of days it'll be time for my next rebirth – and without all those magical ingredients, my egg will never hatch.' She sniffed. 'And this is my last chance, Skribble said so. He told me it is written in the prophecy that I will never lay another egg!' Tears glittered in her eyes again. 'Oh, dearies, I always got by just fine on my own . . . But now I know there's a chance to have a chick, if I blow it I'm not sure I can go on as the only phoenix in all this big, wide world.' She cradled her unlikely egg and looked imploringly at the Worthingtons. 'Can you help a tired old bird, loveys? Can you make my only dream come true?'

Jess looked at Jason, Michael and Milly in turn. 'Do we need to talk about this?'

Milly hardly seemed to hear her. 'We get to do magic!'

'We get to go to all sorts of cool places,' said Jason.

'And we get away from all the normal boring problems in our lives,' added Michael. 'All that and gold too!'

Fenella crossed her wings and closed her eyes. 'Then . . . what do you say?'

'What can we say?' Jess smiled and looked at the others. 'Except . . . yes!'

Chapter Five

'You mean it?' cried Fenella. 'You'll help me?'
She whooped loudly and took off into the air.
The egg went tumbling. Jason dived forward to
catch it. He missed, and it landed with a *thunk*
on the carpet.

'Oooh!' Fenella flapped down, scooped up her
egg and pressed her beak against it, cooing softly.
'I'm sorry, pet, so sorry . . .'

Jason was cringing. 'Why am I rubbish at
anything sporty?'

'That didn't look like anything sporty to me,
mate,' grinned Michael. Jess gave him a shove.

'Is the egg all right?' asked Milly anxiously.

'Right as pie, I'm sure.' Fenella held the egg to
her ear and shook it vigorously. Then, apparently
satisfied, she tucked it firmly under her wing.
'And with you lovely little quacklets questing
away for my special ingredients so bravely . . .'

She shot a loving look at Michael. 'Well! I've got a real fighting chance of hatching it!'

'You can stay here while we're away,' declared Milly. She liked the idea of having a pet phoenix in the den.

'It's a bit chilly, lovey,' Fenella said kindly. 'And as I get closer to my next "becoming", I'm going to need as much heat as possible for the egg and me.'

'We could wrap you in blankets?' Jason suggested.

'Or get the hot-air blower from the loft,' said Michael.

Fenella gave a tinkling laugh. 'I'm talking about real heat, my dears. *Fiery* heat!'

'What about an oven?' Milly suggested.

'Yeah, I can see Dad and Ann asking a phoenix to shift every time they put in the oven chips!' Michael said.

'Oh, they wouldn't see me if I didn't want them to,' Fenella assured him. 'I can make myself completely undetectable to anyone I choose.'

Michael was impressed. 'You can?'

'Truly! It's a little knack I evolved,' Fenella confided. 'Being a unique and magical bird I attract all kinds of interest, and not all of it welcome. Hunters, tourists, cults of phoenix-worshippers . . . they've all pursued me over the years. So I've learned to hide myself from those I don't want to see me, while staying in plain sight for those I do.'

Jess smiled uncertainly. 'You can't, can you?'

Fenella's eyes twinkled. 'A little demonstration, lovey?'

'Hey, she's gone!' Jason declared.

Michael frowned. He could see Fenella plainly. 'No she hasn't!'

'She has, though!' Milly laughed, and Jess nodded, reaching out with her hands uncertainly as if she really couldn't see Fenella.

The phoenix hopped quietly out of the way of Jess's fingers and winked at Michael. 'They can't see me and they can't hear me either!'

'What, really?' Michael watched the others' faces for any signs this was a wind-up, but found none.

Fenella chuckled. 'And now you can't either!'

With that, she disappeared.

'Whoa!' said Michael. 'Where'd you go?'

The beanbag shifted on the floor a little – and suddenly Fenella shimmered back into sight. 'Here I am!'

'Wow,' said Milly. 'That's amazing!' Michael, Jason and Jess nodded eagerly.

'Shame it doesn't really solve the problem of where we can hide you,' said Jess thoughtfully. 'Even if you're not noticed, people would keep turning off the oven.'

'If only we had a spare oven,' said Jason.

'I know!' Milly gasped. 'Mr Milton's old workshop! It's got a kiln that gets ever so hot – and he never uses it – that's why he let Ann and me use it instead!'

'A kiln!' Fenella beamed. 'For firing pots? That people hardly ever use? Sweet heavens in flight, that sounds right up my street.'

'And I'm supposed to be taking Milly there today in any case to pick up those pots she and Mum did,' Jess realized with a grin. 'That's a perfect excuse to go there.'

'So what are we waiting for?' said Michael. 'Let's go!'

'Ooh!' Fenella swept one wing to her breast. 'Such energy! Such resourcefulness! Such courage!'

'Er . . . Michael!' Milly called.

'Yeah, what?' he said, stopping, his dressing gown flapping around his legs.

Milly grinned. 'Maybe we should get dressed first!'

Half an hour and four bowls of gulped-down cornflakes later, the Worthingtons stepped out of the house into the mid-morning sunshine.

'With weather like this,' said Michael, 'we'll have no trouble finding a shaft of sunlight from tomorrow.'

'I hope we can start today,' said Milly longingly.

Jason nodded. '*I* hope this workshop place works out OK for Fenella.'

'Where is she?' Milly wondered. They'd left their new friend to make her own way out of the den window. 'Perhaps she's turned invisible?'

The phoenix suddenly flapped into view. She landed heavily in a tree, sending two plump woodpigeons clattering from its branches. 'Sorry, loveys!'

'Or perhaps not,' said Michael.

'Oh, but I *will* be invisible, my little goslings,' Fenella called. 'To anyone but you. Come on then, lead on!'

Jess looked at Milly. 'You do remember the way to Mr Milton's, don't you?'

'I went in the car with Ann last time,' Milly recalled, 'but I think if we go up the road away from town and then cut through the churchyard and out along the footpath, that should get us there.'

They set off, Fenella flying above them, her egg tucked precariously under one wing, singing a song about a horse-chestnut tree.

'I love singing too!' Milly called. 'I'm hoping to be the star of a show. Only a local one—'

'Milly, shhh!' Jess looked around anxiously. It was hard to believe that passers-by wouldn't notice the big, golden turkey-shaped bird flapping along, singing at the top of her lungs. 'Michael,' she whispered, lagging behind Jason and Milly. 'You do think Fenella's invisibility charm is working, don't you? I mean, she's a bit scatty, isn't she? What if she's got it wrong?'

'Guess we won't know until someone else comes along,' said Michael grimly. A gang of boys bustled into view round the corner of the street ahead of them. 'Look, we can test it— Oh, no!' He broke off, stumbling to a halt and looking horrified. 'No, please, no!'

Jess caught her breath. The people coming down the hill were Michael's friends, Josh, Sam and Thomas – and with them was the new boy-heartthrob, Rick. He was laughing with Sam and elbowing Thomas in the ribs.

'This is a disaster!' Michael hissed.

'Don't be daft, Michael – my magic's still working.' Fenella swooped merrily down straight towards the gang of boys, and not one of them so much as blinked. She flew back up to the nearest tree. 'Ta-daaa!'

Jess smiled. 'Panic over!'

'The disaster I was talking about was being seen out with my little sister, stepbrother and uncool older stepsister,' Michael muttered. Jess elbowed him in the ribs, but he hardly felt it. What were his friends doing out together, anyway? He hadn't known they were meeting up – especially not with Rick.

'Hey, Michael!' called Josh.

'Hi,' said Michael.

Rick threw a look at Milly and Jason. 'Off on a nursery school outing, are you?'

For a moment Michael wondered wildly if he could deny all association with Jason and Milly. But Milly threw Rick a withering look. 'Oh, ha, ha. Very funny. Come on, Michael, we're busy.'

'Oh yeah?' said Josh. 'What you up to?'

Michael shrugged. 'You know. Stuff. What about you?'

'We were just going into town,' said Thomas.

Michael felt his cheeks prickle. So they'd been about to go into town, but without him.

'We tried giving you a ring,' said Josh, looking awkward. 'But there was no answer.'

Yeah, right, thought Michael.

'Do you want to come with us then?' Rick said.

'We've got to go, Michael!' Milly insisted.

Michael ran his hand through his hair, trying to act cool, but it was hard with Milly tugging at his shirt.

To Michael's relief, Jess came to his rescue. 'Hey, let's get a move on, you two,' she said to Jason and Milly. 'Michael can catch us up.' Michael's eyes caught hers. *I owe you one*, he told her silently.

'So, what are you doing then?' Rick said, a faint challenge in his voice. 'Can you come with us to town?'

Michael gritted his teeth. 'My, uh . . . my

stepmum laid a load of errands on me 'cause I broke so many rules this week.'

'Cool,' said Josh.

'Never mind then, mate. Another time,' said Rick easily. 'Hey, I got my allowance today. How about I treat everyone to a burger tonight – end of half-term treat?'

'Cool!' said Josh again, with more enthusiasm, and Sam and Thomas nodded.

'Well, Michael?' said Rick.

Michael looked at Rick's clear, confident face and the words came out of him before he could stop himself. 'I'd love to, mate,' he said with a short smile. 'But actually I get my allowance too and *I'd* been planning to treat everyone as a surprise.'

Rick looked taken aback. 'Oh.'

That phoenix better be right about that gold she's going to give us, thought Michael. 'Not just for a burger though,' he went on airily. 'I thought we could go to the new multiplex in Quilborough – tickets, hot dogs and popcorn. The works. All on me.'

His friends stared at him. 'But you only get a rubbish allowance,' said Sam. 'You're always moaning about how skint you are.'

'Well, I got extra this time.' Michael licked his dry lips – Fenella would give him some gold in advance of finding the stuff, he was sure. Then he could trade some in for cash to fund a trip to the multiplex. He'd be loaded! 'I . . . er . . . my parents found another valuable book – *I* found it actually – and so they've given me some of the money.'

'But I thought you broke so many rules you had to do errands?' said Rick.

'Yeah . . .' Michael shrugged. 'I took the errands over a cash deduction. You on for it then?'

They all nodded. 'You bet!' said Sam.

Michael noted Rick's slightly crestfallen face and felt a surge of triumph. 'I'll meet you outside the ticket office at eight, yeah?' he said, lifting his fist and knocking knuckles with the four of them. 'Laters.' Then he mooched off up the hill after Jess, Milly and Jason.

Jess looked at him as he joined them. 'Everything OK?'

'For once, everything's fine,' said Michael. And he meant it. A grin spread across his face as Fenella launched herself from her branch and swooped off over their heads. Maybe having a talking phoenix in their lives wasn't going to be such a bad thing after all . . .

Chapter Six

After fifteen minutes of walking, the Worthing-tons reached the footpath that bordered the large country house where Mr Milton lived. The gardens of the house were separated from the footpath by a wooden fence and a hedge but at different points along the path the hedge was sparse and it was possible to see into the gardens.

The house was old and rambling. Around the back of it there were massive French windows, and grand stone steps led down from a large patio into the gardens. Bushes cut into the shapes of animals, and mossy stone statues were dotted here and there. The lawns near the house were mown short with neat flowers in beds but further away from the house there was a wood and an orchard.

Michael whistled. 'The old geezer must be worth a fortune to have a place like this.'

'Come on,' said Milly. 'The workshop isn't far from the main drive round the front. Let's see if it's any good.' The others followed her down the footpath, along the road and into the mouth of a grand driveway that led into the landscaped grounds, while Fenella flapped about in the treetops.

'May I help you?' The warm voice was gentle but it made Jess jump all the same. She and the others turned to find a short, slightly tubby man with thinning grey hair emerge from a nearby line of rose bushes, watching them with a quizzical smile. It was hard to tell his age. His face was lined and his back a little stooped, but his eyes seemed bright and youthful.

'Mr Milton!' cried Milly.

'Why, it's Milly Worthington, isn't it?' said Mr Milton, a twinkle in his eyes. 'You'll be here to collect those pots you fired, I'll be bound, with your . . . friends?'

'Family,' said Milly. 'Michael, Jason and Jess.'

Mr Milton nodded his head at each of them in turn. 'I'm pleased to meet you. I'm afraid it's not often I have so many visitors come to call.' He paused, and his smile grew hopeful. 'Are the rest of you interested in pottery too?'

'Sort of,' said Jason cautiously.

'We wondered if we could have a quick look round the workshop,' Jess added.

'Of course!' Mr Milton nodded enthusiastically. 'I'll show you.'

As Jess and the others followed him into the gardens, Jess's eyes fell on a few of the nearby statues. They were all carved in a similar style. One looked like an enormous gargoyle perched on a stone pillar. She looked across the lawn and saw a stallion rearing up, its mane and tail flowing behind it. Nearer the house were two creatures that looked to be half-lion, half-bird. They were fighting, locked in combat.

'Have you had these statues long?' Jason wondered.

'I made them myself,' said Mr Milton shyly. 'Many moons ago now.'

Jess was impressed. 'Really?'

'I used to be a very busy artist indeed.' The old man seemed pleased by her interest. 'I'm afraid my hands are a bit wobbly now, so I stick to restoring my statues to their original glory.'

'Like that one!' Jason exclaimed.

Jess saw he was pointing to a statue of a beautiful woman in the centre of the garden. She stood spotless and white in the centre of a circle of stone, surrounded by stone benches. 'It looks brand new and so real. Look at her face.'

'I often do,' Mr Milton confided. 'It makes me feel less lonely.' He gazed sadly at the statue for some time, apparently forgetting the children were there.

This guy's fruit loops, Michael thought. *Maybe we should go someplace else.*

'Was she someone you knew?' asked Milly politely.

'I did know her very well . . .' Suddenly Mr Milton roused himself, looking reassuringly normal and friendly again. 'Sorry. You must forgive an old man and his memories. Oh, it *is* nice to have visitors. Now, come! Let me show you that workshop . . .'

The children followed him into the small brick building. It was very warm inside. There was an electric oven built into the far wall with an old metal door. On the left side of the room there was a wide stone shelf that ran the length of the building with dusty bags of clay underneath and some pottery tools on top, and on the right side of the room there was a potter's wheel and a stone bench – with some basic pots piled up waiting to be glazed.

'Wow!' said Milly, rushing to see. 'They look all right, don't they?'

'Indeed they do.' Mr Milton beamed. 'You have natural ability, Milly.'

'There you go, sis,' said Michael. 'When you flunk your *Annie* audition you can make pots instead!'

Milly glared at him, but broke off when Fenella swooped down and hovered in the open doorway. 'Oh yes!' the bird cooed rapturously. 'Feel the warmth!'

Jason fanned his face nervously. 'Have you been making something today, Mr Milton?'

'Oh, no. Like I say, wobbly hands.' Mr Milton shrugged; he seemed a little embarrassed. 'I was tinkering with the controls after you came with your stepmother, Milly, and I'm afraid they jammed on. I can't turn off the kiln. I've called someone to fix it but they can't come for a week.'

'Perfect!' Fenella whooped, flying in above their heads. 'I'll be done with it by then. It's fate!'

Jess tried to stifle a smile and Mr Milton looked at her quizzically – of course, he'd seen and heard nothing at all. 'It seems a shame to waste all that electricity,' she said carefully. 'Perhaps we could *all* have a go at potting?'

'Well, you appear to be sensible children . . .' The old man beamed. 'So long as you don't use the kiln without adult supervision, you're welcome to come here whenever you wish.'

'Really?' Milly couldn't help sharing an excited glance with Fenella. 'And would it be OK if we . . . left anything here between visits?'

'Of course! You don't want to be lugging pots and clay and goodness knows what all over the place. Leave whatever you like. Treat the place as your own.' Mr Milton walked to the doorway and Fenella quickly fluttered aside. 'Now, I'm afraid I must leave you for a while. I have an elderly guest staying who's dreadfully fussy.' He chuckled and nodded to himself. 'I'd better attend to him before I get back to my garden. See you again, children. Take care.' With a last little smile, he hobbled off.

The four children held their breaths until he was a safe distance away and then let out their laughter and relief as Fenella came spiralling inside.

'I'm home!' she declared, grabbing the handle to the kiln door with her golden talons. She tugged it open and a wave of intense heat swept through the workshop. 'Ooooh, heaven,' she said, nuzzling inside and placing her egg on the gritty oven floor. 'Cosy as crumpets. This is just the place for me, loveys – thank you! Thank you!'

'Thank old Milton,' said Michael, wiping sweat from his forehead. 'Amazingly lucky though, isn't it – the perfect place falling into our laps? I mean, talk about mega-coincidence.'

'It's *destiny*!' Fenella declared dramatically.

Jason nodded. 'Mr Milton gave us permission to leave things here *and* we can come back whenever we want!'

'We'll have to tell Mum she can't come for a week,' Jess realized. 'But she'll probably be too tied up at work to play with pots anyway.'

'I'm glad Mr Milton has got someone staying with him,' said Milly. 'He smiles a lot but he does seem sad.'

'He's weird,' Michael declared.

'He's just a bit eccentric I think,' said Jess. 'Artists often are, aren't they? He's really talented, though. Did you see those fighting bird things?'

'Gryphons, dearie,' put in Fenella. 'I once knew a gryphon. George, his name was. Slightly grumpy but lovely all the same.' She laughed warmly. 'I'll cheer up that nice Mr Milton when I'm done here, never you fret. He reminds me of somebody . . . Alfred the Great! That was it. He was a great one for roses, was Alfred.'

'What?' Jason stared. 'You knew Alfred the Great?'

'Who d'you think taught him to sing? Without me he'd never have been able to sneak into the Viking camp disguised as a minstrel and learn their plans.' Fenella ruffled her feathers. 'Oh, I've known them all, my pet, the great and the good. And I'll leave *Milton* the Great some lovely phoenix gold when all this is over to say thank you for my bed and board!'

Milly smiled and stroked her back. 'You're so nice.'

'Ooooh!' Fenella rustled her feathers. 'That's what I call nice!' She blinked up at Milly through her long eyelashes. 'I do like my head being scratched too . . .'

'OK.' Milly giggled and scratched the bird's head. Fenella cooed and clucked. 'Jess, come and stroke her too!'

Jess gently brushed her palm against the phoenix's wings. Fenella went into a paroxysm of tweeting and twittering.

'Sorry to interrupt the stroke-fest,' said Michael, 'but isn't it about time we got cracking on this quest of yours? And any chance of some gold up front?'

'Michael!' Milly chided.

'Oh, lovey,' said Fenella, sighing as Jess tickled her chin. 'I only wish I could oblige you. But I'll need some of tomorrow's sunshine first.'

'Of course.' Jason showed Michael the map and pointed to the first instruction. *'You must capture a shaft of tomorrow's sunshine and spin that glorious light into golden thread.'*

Michael frowned. 'Yeah, but how can we really get sunlight from tomorrow? That's impossible.'

'Not with phoenix magic, it isn't.' Fenella's blue eyes were agleam. 'My feathers can be used to travel into the past, present and future. A single one can take you back to any point in my current life and to anywhere in the world I could reach. Or to whisk you off to any point in this body's personal future.'

63

'What?' asked Milly, looking confused.

Jason frowned. 'I think I get it. We can use your feathers to go into the past or into the future but only in your current life span. So if it's about a thousand years since you were last reborn, we can't go back further than that. And we can't go forward past the time of your next rebirth.'

'Exactly, pet!' Fenella nodded. 'I couldn't have put it better myself. And to get the ingredients in the prophecy, you will need to travel not just from here to Cairo, Peru and the Summit of Mount Quamquangle but through the past, present and future as well.'

The Worthingtons exchanged looks. 'Wow! Imagine going back into the past,' said Jason. 'Seeing things as they really were . . .'

Jess grinned. 'Maybe it'll help with my history exam!'

'I want to go into the future and see what happens to us!' said Milly.

Michael's eyes lit up. 'And never mind the gold – if we go into the future, I want to find out tonight's lottery numbers!'

'That's an idea,' said Jess excitedly. 'We can all be rich!'

'Er, just a minny-mo, loveys,' Fenella called over their excited chatter. She looked somewhat apologetic. 'Magic like mine doesn't come without a couple of ground rules, I'm afraid. And one of them is that my powers cannot be used to change the future or the past. It's too dangerous.'

'How can us lot becoming mega-rich be dangerous?' Michael protested.

'Time is like a giant birdbath,' announced Fenella. 'Every decision we make sets the water rippling. So if you jump into the future and decide to cheat, you start a dirty great ripple rippling in the middle of an *existing* ripple . . .' Her eyes glazed over. 'Oooh, it gets ever so complicated.'

But Michael wasn't ready to give up yet. 'Look, surely if we—'

'No, no, NO!' cried Fenella, an unexpected passion in her voice. 'If it were safe to part the mysterious curtains of time, don't you think I'd have gone back to the past and stopped myself from losing my last egg? Or found out what happened to the poor thing at the very least?' She calmed down, seeming to deflate a little. 'But I couldn't. It's impossible. What's done is done, and what shall be, shall be.' She sighed, and placed a claw on her egg. 'I'm only sending you off now because the genie prophecy says these things *must* be acquired. Wise genies like Skribble can read the fates far better than an old bird like me.'

'Don't be upset, Fenella,' said Milly. 'We'll be good.' She looked pointedly at Michael. 'Won't we?'

'Especially since we have to be sixteen or over to win the lottery anyway!' Jason added.

Michael grimaced. 'Well, I guess there's always the phoenix gold! That's got to be better than winning any lottery.'

'Exactly, lovey! Now . . .' The phoenix reached down and carefully selected a long, glowing feather from her chest with her beak. 'You will need one of these for every journey you take, whether past, present or future.'

Jason looked closely at it. 'There's something stuck to that feather.'

Fenella smiled and transferred the feather into her claw. 'It's the tear I cried earlier. When it hit my plumage, the heat fused it into a glow-jewel.' She smiled. 'Place the jewel in a ray of sunshine and it will draw in the light for me to spin into gold. It must be a nice, strong, bright ray of sunshine, mind.'

Michael reached out for the feather eagerly but Fenella snatched it away. 'Remember! Time travel must not be undertaken lightly! Each feather can be used for one day only.' She surveyed each child with her glittering eyes. 'You must always return by sunset, and always keep the feather with you. Because without it, you will be trapped. Trapped!'

'We'll be careful.' Milly's eyes shone. 'This is so exciting!'

Jason nodded.

'Here you are.' Fenella solemnly held the feather out to Michael in her claw. 'Use it well. I'll wait here with my egg, nice and undetectable.'

Michael took the feather. 'At last!' The feather felt hot to his touch, and smelled like old coins. The others crowded round. 'How does it work?' Michael asked Fenella.

'You each take hold of the feather – all of you, that's very important, we don't want anyone left behind, do we?' Fenella clucked. 'Say the words, *Time before me, take me on* followed by the date you want to go to. When you want to return you say, *Time of yore, be never gone.* But be careful. A feather can only take you on so many journeys before it runs out of time-puff.'

'Time-puff,' Michael echoed. 'That's the technical term, is it?'

Fenella fluttered her eyelashes. 'I believe so.'

'Sounds simple enough,' said Jess, taking a deep breath. 'And we only want to travel into tomorrow. Twenty-four hours.'

Michael nodded and held out the shimmering quill. 'Come on, guys,' he whispered. 'Let's do this.'

Cautiously, they all reached out to touch the feather.

'After three,' Jess said, a feeling of warmth flooding through her fingers. 'You say it, Michael. One, two, three . . .'

'Time before us, take us on!' cried Michael. 'Twenty-four hours from NOW!'

Chapter Seven

The world blurred into a golden haze. Milly felt herself whirling round and round. Faster and faster she went until abruptly she stopped. As her feet thumped into the ground, she blinked and looked into the others' shocked faces.

'Whoa. Now that was seriously freaky,' said Michael, giving his head a shake.

Jess looked around the overheated workshop. 'Are we in the future? It all looks exactly the same.'

Milly caught her breath. It *was* all the same but just slightly different. 'The pots have gone!' she exclaimed.

'And look at the rain.' Jason pointed out of the open door. 'It was sunny a moment ago!'

'And look what else,' said Michael, pointing to the ledge. 'Fenella's gone too.' He carefully opened the kiln door, and a blast of heat escaped. The egg sat safely inside, but Fenella was nowhere to be seen.

Milly looked worried. 'What's happened to her?'

'She said she was going to stay undetectable,' Jason reminded her. 'She probably wants to stay out of our way. After all, it could be dangerous to meet us in the future.'

Michael frowned. 'What are you on about?'

'We've jumped a day ahead of ourselves in time,' Jason reminded him. 'We were standing in Saturday, and now it's Sunday. When we go back, we'll jump back to Saturday and tell Fenella all about our adventures. Which means the Fenella here with us on Sunday will know if we succeed or not.'

'All the more reason she *should* be here then,' said Michael.

Jason shook his head. 'If we only know what to do because Fenella tells us now on the Sunday – and *she* only knows because we told her what we did when we go back to Saturday – then . . .' He puffed out his cheeks and let out a long breath. 'Well, it's sort of impossible, isn't it?'

'It's called a time paradox,' said Milly. 'Paradoxes are bad. I saw it on *Doctor Who*.'

'Looks like we'll have to do things the hard way then,' said Michael.

'Maybe harder than we think,' said Jess. 'That rain's pretty heavy. And if there's no sun we can't get the ray of tomorrow's sunshine that Fenella needs.'

'What are we going to do?' Milly said.

'Wait a minute,' said Jason thoughtfully. 'What about today's tomorrow?'

The others looked confused.

'The map didn't say *which* tomorrow we had to get a ray of sunshine from,' Jason explained. 'Every day in the future is a tomorrow!'

Michael clapped Jason on the back. 'You're right! We just keep going forward day by day until we find us some sunshine.'

'Of course!' Relief flooded Jess's face.

Milly took hold of the feather again, and the others followed suit. 'What are we waiting for?'

'*Time before us, take us on!*' Michael declared. 'Another twenty-four hours!'

There was the same feeling of whirling round in a golden haze and the same thump of their feet into the ground as they stopped. They all looked around.

'It's not raining but there's still no sun,' Jess observed, looking out at the overcast sky.

'What did we expect?' sighed Michael. 'It's summer in England. Of course there's no sun.'

'Maybe it comes out later,' Jason mused. 'Can I say the spell?' Michael nodded. '*Time before us, take us on – six hours from now!*'

The shimmer and the spin rippled through them. Jason imagined they were grains of sand falling through golden waters . . .

His excitement ebbed as he opened his eyes and found it was raining again outside.

'We'd better be careful,' said Milly anxiously. 'The feather might run out of time-puff if we use it too often.'

'And we mustn't forget what time it was when we left,' Jess added. 'If we lose track of when sunset is, we'll be stuck here!'

'Uh-oh. Look.' Michael held out his wrist. 'My watch isn't working.'

Jason frowned. 'Well, it was about eleven a.m. when we left Saturday . . . So with all the jumps, and since we've only been here five minutes, now it must be about five thirty-five on Monday afternoon.'

'We'd better keep going,' said Jess. 'Let's jump a few days, Michael.'

Michael cleared his throat as they all touched the feather again. '*Time before us, take us on* – forty-eight hours from now.'

Onward they whizzed once more. The strange tingling, flying sensation was growing familiar. This time when the world stopped spinning and they landed, they all gasped.

'Sun!' cried Milly, looking out at the cornflower-blue sky. It was streaked with white fluffy clouds and the sun was shining down.

Michael went outside and cautiously tapped the crystal at the base of the feather. 'I guess we just point this into the sunshine and watch it glow.'

'Try it!' Jess urged him.

Michael thrust the crystal up towards the sky. The sun shone down. As it hit the crystal, the jewel started to flicker feebly with light. But as the sun disappeared behind a cloud, the light disappeared too.

'Oh,' said Milly in disappointment. 'The sun mustn't be strong enough.'

'Never mind,' said Jess. 'It will come out again soon. Let's wait for a bit.'

'A bit!' Jason said. 'It's Wednesday. We're in the middle of next week.'

It was a weird feeling. They wandered outside.

Jason immediately noticed something was different. He frowned and then realized what it was. 'The statue of the woman has gone,' he said.

'I wonder what's happened to it,' said Jess.

'Oh, who cares about some old statue,' said Michael impatiently. 'I'm thinking about the gold we'll be getting. What are you going to buy, Jase?'

'I dunno. My own laptop would be cool.' Jason sighed. 'Though I guess football coaching's what I need.'

'I wish I could buy a perfect singing voice,' sighed Milly. 'But seeing as I can't have that, I'm

73

going to get tickets to see the show of *High School Musical* and I'll buy myself some new clothes and I'd like a new riding hat and jodhpurs.'

'Wish money could help me pass my exams,' said Jess.

Michael fidgeted and glanced at his broken watch. 'Come on then, sun.'

'There's a song about the sun coming out tomorrow in *Annie*,' said Milly. 'I'm doing it for my audition.' She looked to the sky, threw her arms wide and started to sing.

'*Milly!*' Jess and Michael exclaimed.

'What?' Milly said in surprise. 'I may as well practise if we're hanging round here. My audition's only four days away and—' She broke off, her eyes widening slightly. 'Four days,' she whispered to herself. 'It's Wednesday – *today!*'

'Wait a sec – sun alert!' The sun poured out through a crack in the clouds, and Michael angled the jewel on the feather towards it. 'Here we go again . . .'

This time, the sunbeam was brighter. But the little glow-crystal barely glimmered.

Milly's forehead crinkled. 'It's still not working!'

'Wait a minute!' cried Jason. 'My magnifying glass! We can use it to focus the sun's rays into the crystal!' He patted his pockets. 'I was using the glass to look at the treasure map this morning and put it in my jeans pocket . . .' He fished inside – but pulled out only a plastic handle. 'Oh no! The glass itself must have snapped off when I fell on the floor, trying to catch Fenella's egg!'

Michael scowled. 'Nice one, doofus.'

'It was a good idea though,' said Milly.

'I wish I had a spare one with me,' said Jason.

'What are we going to do?' frowned Jess. 'We can't keep hopping through time trying to find stronger sunshine – we could run out of feather power and get stuck in the future!'

'And it's getting on for evening,' Milly pointed out. 'The sun will be getting weaker, not stronger.' *And I'm in the church hall even as we speak, doing my audition*, she thought. Would she get the part, or would she fail? Right now, in this future world, she was finding out for real. The thought was like a tickle under her skin.

'Oh, no way!' said Jess suddenly, her attention caught by two figures coming down the stone steps.

'Michael!' Jason squeaked, pointing. 'It's . . . it's us!'

'Me and you, Jase – the next week versions!' Michael blinked. 'Whoa, it's a bit weird to be here and see us over there too, isn't it?'

Jason nodded, dumbstruck. It did feel very odd.

'I wonder what you've been doing inside Mr Milton's house?' said Jess.

'Maybe we've just bought it with all our phoenix gold!' Michael laughed.

'I wonder where *we* are?' said Jess to Milly.

Milly nodded in a preoccupied way. She knew *exactly* where she would be right now. And it was only a five-minute walk from here in the glade to the church hall . . .

The future Michael and Jason walked down the steps and across the grass together. They looked a bit nervous, like they were watching out for someone.

Michael turned to the others. 'Look, this is too good a chance to let pass. Let's go and ask ourselves if we find the sunshine. If we don't, then we might as well head off home.'

'But what if we only head off home because we told ourselves to?' said Jason. 'It's a paradox again!'

'You worry too much. It'll be cool.' Michael clapped him on the back and hurried towards the rose garden. 'Come on, let's go and meet our future selves!'

Jason was about to set off after him when Jess's voice stopped him in his tracks. 'Don't you dare!'

'I – I have to,' Jason said, scurrying away. 'I just thought of something. If Michael's right about those future versions knowing what we need . . .'

Jess groaned. 'Come on, Milly, we'd better make sure they don't do anything too dumb.'

'Um, I think I might just stay here,' said Milly. 'I don't want to risk mucking up the future.'

'Well, just make sure you don't move from this spot,' Jess instructed her. 'We can't go home if we're not all together.'

Milly nodded, and watched Jess turn away. Future Michael and Future Jason were sitting on a bench in the garden, and her Jason and Michael were about to catch them up. *I will stay here*, she thought. Fenella hadn't peeped into the past to see what had happened to her egg. So what right did she have to learn how her audition was going to go?

But Fenella losing an egg was a big event, Milly thought. Me getting to be Annie isn't. And I'll find out anyway in a few days . . .

She hesitated a moment longer. Then she ran towards the fence.

As Jess ran after Jason and Michael, she saw Future Michael and Future Jason staring grimly as their younger selves approached.

'So there we are,' said Future Jason. 'I mean, there *you* are.'

Jason felt a shiver pass right through him. It was like staring at a perfect double of himself. He felt unbelievably creeped out.

'I know you're feeling unbelievably creeped out,' said Future Jason kindly. 'I am too!'

'Don't look so surprised to see me, mate,' Michael told his future self as he closed the distance between them. 'You're me – you must have been expecting this.'

'Smart alec,' Future Michael retorted. 'Actually, I can remember everything you said.'

'Oh, yeah?' said Michael – and Future Michael said it too at exactly the same time. They both laughed in perfect harmony. Jess rolled her eyes.

'Look at this!' Future Michael held out his arm and showed off a long deep scratch.

'Ouch.' Michael winced.

'I'd say watch out for the guy with the sword and half a feather, but what's the point?' said Future Michael. 'You won't.'

'This is tricky, isn't it?' said Future Jason, with a sigh. 'We really can't tell you much. See, you've got to just carry on and do the things you did, otherwise Michael and I won't be in the right position to be here in your future now, and none of this works . . .'

'But tell me,' said Jason. 'Do you have a magnifying glass?'

Jason nodded shiftily. 'Yes, because I remember you asking me. I brought Mark's along. Leave it by the workshop door when you're finished.'

'I will.' Jason took it.

'And to answer your question about will you

or won't you,' said Future Michael, turning back to his younger self, 'Jason's right. I can't tell you a thing. Just let him get on with it.'

'What a cop-out!' Michael complained. 'Don't tell me I actually listened to that dumb bird about changing the future?'

The other Michael's eyes flashed with bitter anger. 'Shut it.' He looked away. 'You don't know what you're talking about.'

'You'd better go,' said Future Jason. 'Take care, and good luck.'

'You're going to need it,' said Future Michael glumly.

Jess started at his tone. 'What's that supposed to mean?'

Future Michael was clearly dying to tell her something. But then Future Jason grabbed him and started to bundle him away.

'Do we manage to get everything for Fenella in time?' Jess called after them nervously. 'And Milly and me – we are all right, aren't we?'

'Right now, you're with her at her stupid audition,' said Future Michael.

'I wish we could tell you everything,' Future Jason called earnestly to Jess, 'but we really can't. Now quickly, you know what to do – get the sunshine and get out of here before we manage to muck up your future, our past and who knows what else!'

'Yes, come on, let's get back to Milly,' urged Jess, feeling strangely disquieted. She supposed that two Michaels and two Jasons side by side were enough to upset anyone.

But as she led the way back to the little garden outside the workshop, a chill ran through her.

Milly had disappeared!

Chapter Eight

Milly raced down the path. The big town clock, towering above the surrounding houses, gave the time as 5.45 p.m. Everyone who had been at the auditions would now be just about to find out what parts they were going to have! *I'll be able to listen in*, she thought.

Her heart pounded as she ran. She knew she had to be careful. If someone noticed that she was both inside and outside the hall . . .

I shouldn't be doing this, she thought. But something seemed to be pushing her on. She *had* to know if she got the part!

She crossed the road and ran up to the gates that led to the church hall. But as she reached them she stopped. There was a group of people waiting outside of the hall, and coming out through the doors were all her friends from the drama group! The auditions must have finished slightly early and the announcement been made. Milly hastily slipped into the cover of the bushes beside the gate – then looked at the doors and caught her breath. Her stomach rolled over as she saw herself standing there – pale and stunned, eyes full of tears.

'Well?'

Milly jumped about a foot in the air as she heard Jess's uncertain voice just in front of her.

Jess – the future Jess – broke out of the crowd of people in the car park and hurried forward. Future Milly hurled herself into her stepsister's arms, tears streaking down her face.

Milly felt sick, like she couldn't remember how to breathe. The look of shock on her future face – and the tears – said it all. *I won't be Annie.* The thought burned in her head. *I was right. I'm not good enough. I'm going to mess everything up.*

Future Jess put her arms around Future Milly. 'It's OK. Don't worry . . .'

It was too much. Milly couldn't bear to see any more. With tears stinging her eyes, she turned and ran back across the road and up the path. Despite everything she'd said to the others, she'd hoped that maybe she *would* be good enough to be Annie. But she wasn't. She climbed back over the fence, a heavy dullness filling her heart. As she approached she saw Jess, Michael and Jason milling around and looking worried.

They know I've gone off somewhere, she realized. *If I tell them what I've seen, I'll never hear the end of it.*

She crept up to a tree, drew on all her acting ability and fixed a bright smile on her face. 'Boo!' she shouted, jumping out from behind it. 'Tricked you!'

'Milly!' Jess complained. 'That's not funny!'

'It's lame,' Michael agreed. But then he froze. The clouds were floating away from the sun, and hard shadows stretched out on the ground behind them.

'Quick!' cried Jess.

Michael pulled the feather with the crystal out of his pocket and held it up to the sky. As the sun hit the top of it, the gem seemed to flare but then the light ebbed away once again. 'It's still not strong enough.'

'Not yet . . .' Jason held up the magnifying glass, angling the sun's rays against the feather and the gemstone. 'But if I use the new magnifying glass to concentrate the sunbeam . . .'

'I think it's working!' whispered Milly.

The little crystal glowed again, more and more fiercely. The light within it suddenly blazed out, blinding white. The Worthingtons all blinked and for a moment each of them saw a bright white gem-shape etched onto the inside of their eyelids. When they opened their eyes again the fierce sun-like blaze had gone but the crystal was glowing and glittering in Michael's hand, golden light swirling round inside it.

They stared in silent awe for a few seconds.

'Result, Jase,' breathed Michael. 'It's worked!'

Jason cheered. 'We've got the shaft of tomorrow's sunlight Fenella needs!'

'Wow!' breathed Milly, her sadness almost forgotten in the excitement of completing Fenella's first magical task.

Michael held out the feather. 'Let's get back to Fenella and let her do her gold-spinning thing!'

The Worthingtons hurried back into the shed. Jason set down the magnifying glass outside the workshop door for his future self to collect, as he'd agreed. 'Thank you, me,' he whispered.

Then Michael held the feather out. They all touched it.

Michael took a breath. *'Time of yore be never gone!'*

Milly felt herself swirling round again but this time going in the opposite direction. Golden flashes filled her vision, and the hairs on the back of her neck stood on end. No sooner had the journey begun than it had ended, and a huge relieved screech made her and the others jump into the air.

Fenella was sitting on a workbench, hopping from leg to leg with anxiety. 'Oh, dearies!' she squawked. 'What a relief! Thank goodness you're back safe and sound. All of a quiver I am!'

'Me too,' Milly whispered, thinking back to the scene outside the church hall. 'I'm glad we don't have to go back to the future.'

'What am I like?' Fenella cried theatrically. 'Sending you off like that into goodness knows what!'

'We got your shaft of sunlight!' Jason said eagerly.

'Here,' said Michael, holding up the feather with its swirling, beautiful gemstone. He presented it to her.

'Oh, you wonderful children!' The phoenix took the feather in delight and rubbed her head affectionately against Michael's arm. 'Not that some silly sunlight matters as much as knowing you're all safe of course.' She blinked up at him through her eyelashes.

'We're fine,' Michael said gruffly.

She gave him an expectant look and he tentatively stroked her head. 'Oooh, that hits the spot, lovey, oh, yes . . .'

Michael stroked a bit harder and Fenella, in an ecstasy of being stroked, spun about on the spot – and suddenly her tail burst into flames.

'Whoa!' Michael yelled, leaping backwards.

'Oh, my goodness me,' squawked Fenella in alarm. 'I just can't control my body heat at the moment – I'm like that kiln, you can't turn me off! None of you were hurt, were you?'

Michael sucked his burned fingers. 'Nothing a bit of gold wouldn't cure.'

'Don't be so rude,' Jess hissed.

'That's not rude, Jess lovey, it's forthright!' Fenella winked at Michael. 'Isn't it, my pet?'

Michael grinned and held out the golden feather to the phoenix. The crystal at the base of it glowed and sparkled.

Fenella clapped her wings together. 'A shaft of tomorrow's sunshine – just what the genie egg-doctor ordered!'

'We had to go a few days into the future, is that OK?' asked Jason anxiously, remembering it had been his idea.

'Oh, that's just fine,' said Fenella gaily. 'A ray of sunshine from any old tomorrow will do. Silly me, forgetting to mention that! I don't know what my mind's doing at the moment.' She placed the feather on the workbench beside her. 'Now, gather round, my little ducklings!'

They all moved closer, exchanging looks of anticipation.

Fenella walked once around the feather, rustled her wings and then began to sing. Her voice was beautiful, low and soft, but gradually rising. The crystal started to vibrate, golden light swirling round inside it like a mini tornado. It began to hum.

For a few seconds the phoenix and the crystal held the same note and then Fenella stopped singing and touched her beak to the top of the crystal. It continued to shake and hum and she appeared to pull a long golden strand out of the crystal with her beak. The children watched in astonishment as she pulled more and more of the gold out, passing it down to her left foot and, from there, to her right. Michael couldn't stop staring as Fenella's talons started to flit about in a lightning-quick dance, the gold thread passing from one foot to another almost as if she was knitting at super-speed with her claws. Milly tried to see what she was doing but the phoenix was moving too quickly now, her beak constantly passing down a seemingly endless new supply of the gold thread.

'Look!' Milly breathed as from under Fenella's right claw a small rectangle of smooth gold began to emerge.

'She's turning the thread into solid gold!' whispered Jason.

Fenella glanced at him. '*Weaving* is the correct expression, lovey,' she said, before turning her attention back to the task.

'Whatever it is, it's amazing!' said Jess.

Michael nodded, his eyes fixed on the gold rectangle. 'Awesome . . .'

On and on Fenella went, and soon there was a pile of golden rectangles – each the size and shape of a credit card – and a neatly rolled-up ball of gold string, tied up tightly.

The light in the crystal flickered and went out. Fenella lifted her beak from the stone. She looked proud but tired. 'Phoenix gold!' she said in a low, breathless voice. 'The string's for my nest but the sheets are for you. I said I'd pay you well for your efforts to help me, dearies, and here you are – three bars each. Priceless, they are. Priceless!'

Jess gulped. 'You . . . you don't *have* to pay us, you know.'

Milly nodded. 'We're glad to help you. You're amazing.'

'As are *you*, my pets,' said Fenella with a puffed-out smile. 'It's a pleasure to spoil such deserving young chickadees. Now, don't be shy. Come up and help yourselves!'

'Well, if you insist . . .' Michael stepped up and grabbed three of the little slabs for himself and three for Milly.

Milly took them from him carefully and stared in wonder. Smooth and glowing, each one felt warm and tingly in her hand. As she moved it in the light, it gave off a deep reddish gleam. 'They're beautiful,' she murmured. 'Thank you, Fenella.'

Jason nodded as he counted out three more. 'Yes, thank you.'

'They're gorgeous,' breathed Jess, taking hers.

'It's gold!' said Michael, his eyes gleaming. 'Gold, gold, lovely gold!'

'I could tell you some tales about the times I've been ordered to weave it,' said Fenella, still panting softly for breath. 'I've been captured, held prisoner, deprived of food until I gave in . . . dreadful situations! There was this one time when Sultan Ibrahim the First of the Ottoman Empire caught me in a net . . .' She covered her eyes as if it was too horrible to remember.

'Oh, you poor thing,' said Milly.

'You look worn out after all that weaving,' said Jess. 'You should rest now. We'll come again tomorrow.'

Michael nodded. 'Beats getting ready for school the next day.'

Fenella sighed. 'Oh, you are a tonic, my loves. I'm so pleased I found you. Now I can sleep soundly at night again.' She stifled a yawn with a wing. 'And I *am* rather sleepy.'

'Bye-bye,' Milly whispered, kissing the bird on her head. Jason and Jess stroked her wings, and even Michael patted her awkwardly on the back.

'Bye, loveys.' Her eyes began to close and she flapped clumsily back into the kiln. 'Maybe if I just have forty winks . . .' She tucked her head under her wing, and soon she was snoring softly, glowing in the red heat of the furnace. Jess carefully closed the kiln door.

'Wey-hey – we're loaded!' Michael cried gleefully, starting outside. 'Who needs the lottery? I don't know why I looked so fed up in the future. All we have to do is turn this gold into cash and then the fun really starts!'

'*Fun!* Fun, he says!' A familiar mumbling, grumbling voice broke through the air behind them. The children stared at each other for a long, electric moment. 'I might have known it. I might have expected it . . .'

Milly was first to swing round. Floating round the side of the shed on a little pink cloud was a funny-looking worm with a drooping moustache and a purple genie turban on his head.

'I don't believe it!' she squealed. 'It's Skribble!'

Chapter Nine

Skribble's tiny dark eyes gleamed above his moustache. His segmented body trembled as he bobbed about on the pink cloud.

Jason beamed. 'Skribble, is it really you?'

'Course it is!' A grin spread over Michael's face. 'The grumpiest genie in the world.'

'Grumpy, I? I, who have impressed popes and princes with my sweet nature? Huh!' Skribble looked set for a major huff, but then his expression softened. 'Greetings to you all, my young friends.'

'This is so brilliant!' Milly ran to the cloud and looked at the magical bookworm in delight. 'I've missed you TONS. Where did you come from? What are you doing here? Can you stay?'

Skribble looked a little awkward. 'I'm afraid I cannot, Milly. I have come here to' – he made a strange strangled squawk – 'to . . .' He opened

and closed his mouth, as if struggling for words. 'I . . . I . . .'

The children exchanged looks. Normally, nothing in the world could stop Skribble from speaking.

'What's the matter?' Jason asked.

'The matter?' Skribble blustered. 'Why . . . the only thing that's the matter around here is the four of you and your attitude!'

Jess frowned. 'Pardon?'

'You have all accepted a most vital quest to help that dear phoenix, and time is very short,' said Skribble imperiously. 'I know how easily distracted you all are. Heads full of hessian, the lot of you!' He glanced at Michael. 'I particularly know the effect phoenix gold can exert on the human soul.'

'Are you spying on us?' asked Michael indignantly.

'No, but . . .' Skribble paused, his face contorted as if in pain. 'I must warn you that you must proceed with your good work with all possible speed. There is no time to waste.'

'Are you sure you're all right, Skribble?' Milly frowned.

Skribble looked at her closely. 'You should know by now that where magic is concerned, great danger may be lurking.'

'Danger?' Jason echoed nervously.

'That map, the one I gave Fenella.' Skribble nodded his head towards Jason. 'Do you have it?'

Jason pulled it out of his pocket and unrolled it. 'It's here.'

'Study it well,' said Skribble. 'Look at the map closely. Make sure that you – and Fenella – read and digest every . . . single . . . syllable!' With each word he spoke he bobbed up and down. He looked fiercely at Michael and then back pointedly to the map. Michael followed the direction of the genie's tiny eyes to the words at the bottom: *Know Yourself, Trust Yourself, Believe in Yourself.* 'Think clearly!' Skribble exclaimed, looking back at him. 'Remember what you learned while following *The Genie Handbook,* and heed those lessons well.'

'OK, keep your 'tache on, Worm,' said Michael.

'Are you sure nothing's wrong, Skribble?' asked Milly.

'Wrong? Goodness, no. What could be wrong?' Skribble shook his head. 'Simply remember that there . . . there is always one who watches . . . watches *closely* . . .'

Jess looked uneasy. 'Who?'

'My time has run out. I must leave you!' Skribble gabbled. 'Delay no longer but be careful, dear children – *please* be careful!'

'But Skribble, we know we're all right,' Michael pointed out. 'We've seen ourselves in the future.'

Skribble shook his head. 'Nothing is set in stone where magic is involved.'

'Please, Skribble,' Milly urged him. 'Can't you just tell us who is watching us and—'

'Farewell, my brave friends,' said Skribble. He started to swirl round and round on his cloud, faster and faster. 'Remember what I have told you . . .' With a faint pop, Skribble and his cloud disappeared.

For a moment the four Worthingtons just stood there staring at the empty air where Skribble had been.

'What *has* he told us?' Milly felt utterly baffled. 'Where's he gone?'

'And where did he come from?' said Jason.

Jess frowned. 'It was like he was trying to encourage us and warn us at the same time.'

'*There is one who watches closely,*' Milly quoted with a little shiver.

'Maybe it's Mr Milton,' Michael suggested. 'Spying on us from his rosebushes!'

Jason frowned. 'I wonder what Skribble *did* mean?'

'You know the worm,' said Michael, shrugging. 'He's worse than Milly for making a drama out of nothing.'

'Hey!' Milly protested.

'Anyway, now we've got other things to think about,' Michael went on, pulling his three gold bars out of his pocket. 'Like how to cash these in! The shops are only open for another hour or so. I'm going to go into town right now and see who'll swap this for some real money.'

Milly stared at him. 'You're really going to sell Fenella's gold?'

'Yeah. So what?' Her look of disappointment niggled at him but he refused to show it.

Milly bit her lip. 'But Fenella gave us that gold – it's special, it's amazing, it's . . . from *her*.'

'But I've promised the guys a night out tonight. Look, I won't sell all of it,' Michael countered. 'I just really need some cash if I'm going to get my mates back onside.'

Milly looked sceptical. 'If they were really your mates you wouldn't need to keep them with money.'

'Oh, stick to singing your pukey songs, Annie!' said Michael crossly. 'I'm out of here!'

Without a backward glance he jogged away through the clearing, along the driveway and started heading back into town. But as he ran along the footpath he knew he had only blown up at Milly because she was making sense. Even so, what was he supposed to do – give up and let Rick nick all his friends? He put his hand in his pocket and felt the phoenix gold. *When I buy Rick his hot dog later,* Michael thought, *I hope he chokes on it.*

Thankful that even the shops in Moreways Meet were open till six on a Saturday, he made his first stop at the jeweller's on the High Street. They had a sign in their window that said WE BUY GOLD – perfect!

The woman in the shop was starchy and pale with thick blonde curls. Her cherry-red lips were pursed in disapproval as he wandered up to the counter in his scruffy jeans and football shirt.

'Hi,' he began, trying his most winning smile. 'You buy gold, yeah?'

'Sometimes,' said the woman guardedly.

'You'll want to buy this.' Michael pulled one of the pieces of phoenix gold out and slapped it on the counter.

The woman's eyebrows shot up so far they were almost lost in her hairdo. She picked up the gold and held it to the light, turning it round and looking at it from all angles. It gleamed softly. 'It's beautiful,' she said slowly. 'Like nothing I've ever seen.' Her expression hardened as she turned back to Michael. 'Where did you get it?'

'It used to be my gran's,' he lied. 'She left it to me in her will, and now I need to flog it.'

'Do you, indeed,' the woman said, looking

more closely at the gold. 'Well, it hasn't got a hallmark. It isn't real gold.'

'Course it is,' Michael blustered.

'I'm not sure *what* it is,' she went on, engrossed. 'And besides, you're under eighteen. I'd need your parents' permission to even value it.' She looked at him again. 'I'll give you a form if you like and you can get them to fill it in.'

Michael's palms were sweating. 'Can't you just buy it off me right now? Say, a hundred quid?'

The woman frowned at him. 'Look what's going on? Where did you really get this? What's your address?'

The questions hit Michael like a barrage of bullets. His nerve broke and he snatched the gold back from her and barged back out of the door. *Stupid*, he told himself. *She'll probably call the cops now, thinking you nicked it.*

Quickening his step, he headed towards the dowdy little maze of crooked alleys that led to his back-up plan – the second-hand shop, Junk and Disorderly. It was here that they'd left Skribble in the genie lamp after saying goodbye. It was weird how he had showed up outside Milton's house, waffling on like that.

Michael lingered in the cobbled street outside the junk shop a while and caught his breath. If he looked furtive or anxious, the owner – Barry, his name was – might think the gold was dodgy too. And Michael knew this was his last chance to get a bar cashed in time to hit the multiplex that night.

He pushed open the door. Barry looked up from his dog-eared paperback and nodded vaguely. 'All right, son?'

'It's your lucky day, Barry,' said Michael, slicking back his hair. 'I need some cash, pronto, so I'm having to sell this family heirloom . . .'

He held up the phoenix gold. But the windows were so grimy and the side street so gloomy that little light could sneak in to show its sparkle. Even so, Barry put down his paperback. 'What's that then? It's never gold, is it?'

'It's a special type of gold,' said Michael. 'It was left to me by a long-lost uncle from Cairo . . .'

'Ah.' Barry gave him an indulgent smile. 'Your mum and dad know you're selling it, do they?'

Michael nodded. 'Yeah, course they do.'

'And they thought you'd get the best price for a special type of gold down my old junk shop, did they?' Barry shook his head. 'Sorry, son, I can't touch that for you. If I put a thing like that in my window, I'd have your parents kicking off at me, or the police round asking questions, all sorts of bother.' He picked up his paperback again. 'And I don't do bother.'

'Fine,' Michael retorted, his cheeks burning. 'I'll take it somewhere else and let them have the bargain of the century.'

'Any reputable place will give you the same answer I did, son,' Barry assured him.

Suddenly there was a clatter from the back of the shop. Michael looked over and saw a figure watching him from behind a teetering tower of cardboard boxes. A man in a raincoat, his hair an unkempt grey thatch, his eyes dark and piercing. A metal teapot had just fallen out of a box near his feet.

'Need help with anything, mate?' called Barry.

The man shook his head. But his eyes remained on Michael.

A shiver tangled through Michael's bones. *'There is always one who watches,'* Skribble had said. For a moment Michael was put in mind of the two genies from the Genie Council who'd come after them in search of their magical handbook. The scruffy man didn't look like the slick, smartly dressed genies but there was something strangely similar about his sharp, dark gaze . . . And Jess and Milly had seen those genies first in this very junk shop.

Michael turned and stormed out without another word. Once outside he ran along the zigzagging alleyway and onto the main road, his heart pounding. But there was no sign that he was being followed, and once back on the sunny, milling High Street, his fears soon faded. But his money worries did not.

'Dumb phoenix,' he muttered to himself as he ran along the street. 'Unless I can come up with some cash before eight o'clock, I'm doomed!'

Jason lay on his bed, still turning his gold over in his hands. The whole day had been unbelievable, and it was all he could do not to run around babbling about it to anyone who'd listen. *Like anyone would ever believe me*, he thought wryly. *Anyway, it's so cool to have a real, incredible secret* . . . He couldn't wait to go on their next magic mission the next day.

Suddenly there was a pounding on the stairs, and the next moment Michael burst in through the bedroom door. He looked out of breath and his hair was spiked up with sweat. 'Jase, mate,' he panted. 'How much cash have you got on you?'

'Huh?' Jason frowned. 'Didn't you sell your gold then?'

'I couldn't! No one would take it off me.' He got down on his knees in front of the bed. 'I'm begging you, Jase, old buddy – lend us your cash.'

'But I haven't got much,' Jason protested. 'I paid some into my savings account last week.'

'That's not fair!' Michael groaned. 'If you've got enough to put in a savings account, you should let me have some!' He slumped down on Jason's bed. 'It's hopeless. I said I'd pay for Rick, Josh, Sam and Thomas to go to the multiplex tonight, with hot dogs, popcorn, the works. I thought I'd be quids in after helping that crazy bird. Instead, I've got as much cash as I had this morning – one pound thirty-eight.'

'I've got three pounds you can borrow,' Jason offered.

'That's, like, three quarters of one hot dog.' Michael shook his head. 'What am I gonna do? Dad won't give me another loan. Even if he did, I'd be paying it off for ever.'

Jason shrugged. 'Pretend to be sick.'

'I've made the offer now,' said Michael miserably. 'They'll expect me to treat them when I'm better 'cause I told them I got all this money . . .'

'So tell them you lost it,' said Jason.

Michael looked at him suddenly. 'Tell them?' He smiled and shook his head. 'Better than that – I'll *show* them I lost it. With a little help from you, mate.'

'From me?' With dread, Jason recognized the smile on Michael's face as one that meant an 'amazing' plan had just occurred to him.

'Come on!' Michael bounced off the bed and dragged Jason to his feet. 'Milly's not the only one in this family who can put on a performance – and here's where I get to prove it!'

Michael swung his rucksack onto his shoulder and jumped down from the bus as it shuddered to a stop round the corner from the multiplex. Jason was right behind him. They were the only two getting off.

'Thanks for funding our bus tickets, Jase,' said Michael. 'So, this is Quilborough. Well, at least no one knows us.'

'What difference does that make?' asked Jason. 'What are we doing here – and why did you tell Mum and Mark that you were taking me to see a film? Jess and Milly are completely suspicious. They *know* you never normally take me out with your mates.'

'Sorry, Jase – afraid it's just not cool to let little brothers or stepbrothers tag along.' Michael smiled craftily. 'But cheer up, I *will* be spending the whole evening with you tonight. Because you're going to mug me.'

Jason stared. 'I'm *what?*'

'It's the obvious solution,' said Michael. 'I turn up at the pictures all roughed up with my pockets torn, and tell the lads someone nicked all my money. That way they won't expect me to treat them all another time.'

'But then Rick will treat them all instead.' Jason

scratched his head. 'That's what made you say you'd treat everyone in the first place!'

'Yeah, but at least the lads will know I made the bigger offer and he's being forced to match it,' said Michael. He set off down a quiet close leading off from the main street. 'Come on, this looks like a good enough place.'

Jason reluctantly followed. 'I still don't get why you need me along.'

'I don't want to spend a Saturday night hanging around all by myself, do I?' Michael patted his rucksack. 'Anyway, I need you to wait back here with my spare clothes. Obviously I can't go back looking like I've been mugged – Dad and Ann would freak and call the police or something. So I just pop down, do my acting bit, tell them I'm all shaken up and that I hope they have a good time without me and push off back here. Then you and me kill time till it's time to go home and we tell Dad and Ann we've been to the film.'

'That's a lot of lying,' said Jason doubtfully.

Michael knew he was right but forced himself not to dwell on it. He scowled – and suddenly threw himself into a flowerbed.

Jason stared. 'Michael, are you OK?'

'I'm just roughing myself up a bit,' Michael told him. 'Come on, try and rip the back of my shirt.'

'But that'll ruin it!' protested Jason.

'Stop being such a girl!' Michael was rubbing mud on his face and into his hair.

Sighing, Jason grabbed a handful of Michael's shirt and tugged on it with all his strength. The fabric stretched but wouldn't tear.

'Come on, put some effort in!' Michael strained to pull away from him to make Jason's task easier but only managed to overbalance him. He fell on top of Michael and forced his head into a rose bush.

'Sorry!' said Jason. 'Oh no, the thorns have scratched you.'

'Have they?' Michael grinned. 'Cool! More realistic.' After a few minutes wrestling with clothes and handfuls of mud, Michael deemed himself ready for his star turn. With a cheery wave, he left his stepbrother with his holdall and jogged off towards the multiplex to make his dramatic entrance. He turned into the car park, ignored the curious looks from the people he pushed past. Aha – there were his mates, laughing at something Rick the Slick was saying. He quickened his pace, tried to get himself into the right mood of desperate horror. *It can't be true! But it is! All my money's been—*

'Stolen!' he gasped, staggering up to Thomas, Josh and Sam. 'My lovely cash – nicked!'

His mates spun round and stared at him uncomprehendingly. For a long, horrible moment Michael was certain they knew he was lying. But then Rick of all people put an arm around his shoulder. 'Easy, mate,' he said, looking genuinely worried. 'Come on, lean on me. What happened?'

'This big guy,' Michael gasped, pulling carefully free of Rick's grip. 'Came up behind me and knocked me to the ground. Look at the state of me . . .'

Now his mates started forward, their faces full of concern. Michael felt a twinge of guilt for tricking them like this. But it was too late to back out now.

'Don't crowd him, guys, give him some room,' ordered Rick. 'Come on, Michael, we've got to get you down the cop shop. Maybe the hospital. Forget the film. I'll ring for my dad to get us.'

'Er, no!' said Michael in alarm. 'It . . . it's not worth bothering anyone.'

'What are you on about?' said Josh. 'If some nutter's running about—'

'Yeah, but he's gone now, with all my cash.' Michael shrugged. 'We'll never find him.'

'Hello, Michael!' Michael turned to find a woman in her fifties with long grey hair and large glasses walking towards him. He cursed – it was Dad's friend Ginny from the newsagent's. 'I saw you playing with your little brother as I drove past just now – just look at the state of you!'

Josh frowned. 'You were with Jason? Well, where is he?'

'Um . . .' Michael felt his heart plummet into his stomach – the impact turning his face bright red. 'No, I wasn't with—'

'I saw him jump on you, pulling your shirt.' Ginny smiled and shook her head. 'Little monkey! No wonder you look such a state. Well, enjoy your film, boys. Cheerio!'

'He wasn't . . . I mean, he . . .' Michael looked at his puzzled mates. 'That is, I . . .'

Rick spoke slowly. 'You were mugged by your little brother?'

'No!' Michael squeaked. 'No, she got it all wrong!'

Thomas started to grin. 'Mate, that's shameful.'

'I was just teaching him how to fight,' Michael protested, 'when suddenly—'

'Why would you be teaching him to fight out in Quilborough when you'd come to see a film with us?' Sam grinned. 'He followed you out here, didn't he? He jumped you!'

'Ginny can't see straight,' said Michael angrily. 'Jason could *never* get me.'

Thomas pointed across the car park. 'Then how come you're a total muddy mess and

107

your little stepbro's over there without a mark on him?'

Michael whirled round. Sure enough, there was Jason, peering out from behind a bollard near the car park entrance, watching him like a particularly useless spy.

'He – he's changed his clothes!' said Michael, aware how pitiful the lies sounded. 'Yeah, look, he must have brought some in that rucksack.'

'That's *your* rucksack!' Josh burst out laughing. 'Mate, he nicked your bag too, didn't he?'

Michael cringed. 'No!'

'That is priceless,' Sam guffawed.

'No wonder you didn't want to tell the cops,' Rick added, high-fiving Thomas and Josh.

Michael couldn't take it any more. He turned and marched away, cheeks on fire, his friends' laughter ringing in his ears.

'Oh, come on, Michael, don't be like that,' Thomas called. 'We'll protect you from big bad Jase – and any little old ladies passing by . . .'

'This is a nightmare.' Michael zeroed in on Jason and grabbed him by the arm, dragging him away. 'What are you doing here?' he hissed furiously. 'They saw you! You've ruined everything.'

'Sorry, Michael, but there was this strange guy in a raincoat watching me from down the street,' said Jason worriedly. 'He gave me the creeps.'

'I'm gonna give you a lot more than that!' Michael snatched the rucksack from him. 'We're getting the bus back home right now. I'll get changed and tell Dad the film was full up. But what am I going to say when it starts going around the school that YOU beat me up?' He closed his eyes and groaned. 'Next time we take a phoenix trip somewhere, I'm staying behind!'

Chapter Ten

The next morning, Michael was woken up by the duvet being yanked off him. 'What's going on?' he moaned.

'That's exactly what we want to ask you!' Jess said tartly.

Blinking his eyes open, Michael saw Jess and Milly standing next to his bed. Milly had her hands on her hips; Jess was holding his duvet out of his reach.

'What happened last night, Michael?' Milly demanded. 'Jason won't tell us. What were you up to?'

When he and Jason had got in the night before, Michael had mumbled about the film being full and stomped straight up to his room. He hadn't come out since. Jason had got ready for bed, refusing to say what had happened, but Milly could tell he was upset.

'I just thought Jase could do with a night out,' Michael attempted feebly.

The girls' eyebrows shot up into their hair in disbelief.

'Oh, all right,' Michael mumbled. He shut his eyes as the memories of the night before swept over him, and grudgingly explained what had happened. His cheeks blazed red as he relived the moments, remembered the looks on his mates' faces, Jason standing there, the laughter . . .

'Michael, you . . . you . . . idiot!' Milly shook her head, a small grin catching at the sides of her mouth.

'Don't you dare laugh,' he snarled, snatching the duvet back from Jess.

'I can't believe Ginny saw you!' Jess cringed. 'And she told all your mates. Oh, Michael, you loser!'

He glared at her. 'Thanks for the support!'

'It's Jason I feel sorry for,' said Milly. 'You tried to use him.'

'He wanted to come with me!' Michael hid back under the duvet. Lousy, no-good gold!'

'Lousy, no-good Michael, you mean!' Milly softened her voice. 'Anyway, look. Jess and I talked about stuff last night and we think we should get down to the workshop at eleven.'

Jess nodded. 'I've really got to do some history revision first thing this morning. Though how

I'm going to concentrate knowing we'll be going to—'

'Old Cairo!' Milly's eyes gleamed with excitement. 'I can't wait! I'm going to go to the village hall this morning to try and borrow some costumes from my drama group so we fit in a bit. I think they've got some Egyptian ones that might do.'

'Better than wearing jeans and T-shirts,' Jess agreed.

'If you find a disguise for me, let me know.' Michael poked his head out of the duvet and looked at Jess. 'Can you just imagine what it's going to be like at school tomorrow? My life isn't going to be worth living.'

'True!' Jess grinned unsympathetically. 'Perhaps you should just hole up in Cairo for the rest of your life!'

Michael retreated back under the duvet with a sigh. Right now, he felt the idea had a lot going for it.

A little while later, Milly set off to the village hall with Jason, who'd offered to come with her. She knew that Maureen and Ruby, the two ladies who were in charge of costumes, were going to be at the hall that day, agreeing designs for *Annie*.

She glanced at Jason as they hurried along, hoods pulled up against the drizzling rain. He hadn't said much since they had left the house, so she decided to air what was on *her* mind. 'I can't believe Michael tried to get you to mug him yesterday. What was he thinking?'

'I dunno, but I was rubbish,' Jason said sadly. 'I didn't know what to do and then all his mates saw me. Michael's going to hate me for ever now.'

'Well he shouldn't,' Milly said, looking indignant. 'He should never have said he'd buy all his friends' tickets and everything in the first place and then he should have just told them the truth.' She squeezed Jason's arm. 'It's not your fault, Jase.'

Jason looked at her gratefully. 'Thanks.'

'Anyway, we've got far more important things to think about right now than my dumb brother,' Milly went on. 'We've got to think about how we're going to persuade Ruby and Maureen to lend the costumes to us.'

'We could say that Mum and Mark want to borrow them to promote a book,' Jason suggested.

Milly shook her head. 'Too risky. Ruby and Maureen might go to the shop and ask Dad and Ann why they want them.' She thought again. 'I suppose we could say we need them for a school project?'

'I guess,' said Jason. 'But they're not really going to just lend expensive costumes to two kids, are they?'

'Well, we'll have to go about it the right way,' Milly said, a crafty look stealing into her eyes. As she pulled him into the car park, she stopped in her tracks. She remembered seeing herself coming out of the hall with a shocked face, watching herself sobbing on Jess's shoulder . . .

'Are you all right?' Jason asked her in surprise.

'Yes,' Milly said, trying to force her voice to sound normal. *It's not important now,* she thought. *I'm here because I want to help Fenella. Forget about the auditions. Just think about that.*

Taking a deep breath, she smiled at Jason and led him towards the hall door. 'Come on!'

A middle-aged lady with curly red hair was standing in the hall, putting costumes into piles. A younger woman, a blonde, was helping her.

'Hello, Milly,' the red-haired woman said as Milly opened the door.

'Hi, Ruby!' Milly said with her brightest smile. 'Hello, Maureen. This is my stepbrother, Jason.'

Jason smiled his most trustworthy smile.

'So what are you two doing here?' asked Maureen.

'I knew you were sorting out the outfits and I wondered whether you needed any help,' said Milly. 'Jason said he'd come along too. Didn't you, Jase?'

'Ummm . . . yeah,' Jason agreed.

'That's so sweet of you both,' Maureen said fondly.

'We could certainly do with a couple of extra pairs of hands,' Ruby agreed.

'Oh, thank you!' Milly said, as though sorting costumes was what she loved best in the whole world. 'We're going out at eleven with our family but we'd love to help until then!'

'Well, take your coats off and come over here,' said Maureen. 'We're trying to sort out costumes for the dancers in the chorus. A lot of stuff obviously isn't suitable and a lot needs chucking . . .'

Jason took an armful of clothes with an embarrassed nod. He sorted uncertainly through a ragbag bundle of old outfits while Milly chattered away to the ladies. After several minutes Milly casually crossed to a big wardrobe. 'Oh, wow!' she exclaimed suddenly. 'You've got some Egyptian costumes! We're doing an assembly about the Egyptians at school, me and Jason and two friends.' Milly pulled out a couple of hangers loaded with white folds of fabric. 'We're supposed to be dressing up but we're just using old sheets.'

Jason saw Ruby and Maureen exchange looks.

Milly touched one of the costumes very carefully. 'These are so beautiful. Our teacher would be so amazed if we had something like this.' She smiled sadly at Jason. 'Oh well, the sheets will be fine . . .'

'You could always borrow these, Milly dear,' said Maureen.

Ruby nodded. 'How long would you need them for?'

'I could bring them back tomorrow, after school,' said Milly quickly.

Ruby smiled. 'Well, we wouldn't lend our costumes to just anyone but I'm sure you two will take very good care of them.'

'We will! We promise!' Milly said eagerly.

'We've got sashes and robes that go with them. somewhere,' added Maureen.

'Oh, thank you!' Milly hugged her. 'It's so kind of you!'

Maureen looked very pleased. 'It was kind of you to offer to help, dear. And one good turn deserves another, I always think.'

Milly looked at Jason, who was standing there speechless – and grinned.

A little while later, Jason and Milly headed up the drive of Mr Milton's house with four carrier bags full of Egyptian costumes, belts, turbans and head-scarves.

'We're bound to fit in when we go back to Egypt now,' said Milly, bubbling with enthusiasm.

They reached the workshop. Jess and Michael were already inside with Fenella. Although the weather was cold and wet, it was as boiling hot as ever inside the building. The golden bird was huddled deep inside the kiln on top of her egg, calling out through the open furnace door.

'How was I to know you wouldn't be able to sell my gold, duckie?' the phoenix was protesting. 'Merchants today can't have much taste, that's all I can say.'

'And Michael doesn't have much *sense*,' Jess added.

'That's for sure,' said Milly, smiling sweetly at her brother. 'Hello, Fenella. Hi, Jess.'

Jason smiled round at everyone and showed them the carrier bags he was holding. 'We've brought some outfits!'

'Oh, great,' Michael muttered.

'I love a fashion show!' Fenella smiled round at the children, but Milly thought the bird was looking less bright today in every sense. Her golden plumage seemed a little tarnished, and her good humour seemed forced. Milly was reminded of how her stepmum would quietly soldier on when she was ill or had a headache.

'Are you feeling OK, Fenella?' she asked.

'Me, pet?' The phoenix tried to laugh gaily, but began to cough instead. 'Oh, don't you go worrying about me. I'm always a bit wobbly before a rebirth. I confess I don't usually feel quite as bad as this but the swan goes on till she drops, they say – and I'll be blowed if some silly swan's getting one up on a magical bird like me! Now, these outfits of yours . . .'

Milly and Jason emptied the carrier bags out and offered round costumes. Michael studied his suspiciously – a white tunic and baggy trousers made of thin, flimsy nylon with a bright sapphire-blue sash pinned to the waist. 'This looks like a pair of kiddie pyjamas,' he complained.

'They're fine!' Milly said.

Jason pulled on some baggy white trousers over his shorts and looked at himself doubtfully. He felt like he was about to star in a panto!

'Don't you worry, lovey,' said Fenella, seeing his expression. 'Anything goes in old Cairo! It's a real melting pot. And in the height of summer, I mean *really* melting.'

'Were you reborn in the summertime then?' asked Milly.

'By your calendar . . .' Fenella closed her eyes and muttered to herself as she worked it out. 'August the twenty-sixth, 1092.'

'Then we're really going back almost a thousand years to get the ash from your last nest,' Jason breathed.

Michael's frown grew deeper. 'Uh-huh. In a pair of pyjamas!'

'You girls should wear a robe, and a headscarf.' Fenella looked thoughtfully at Jason's straw-coloured mop of hair. 'And you should certainly wear one of those turbans, lovey. That thatch of yours will stand out like a sparrow at a gathering of eagles!'

When they all had their costumes and headgear on, Milly twirled round. 'How do I look?'

'You look pretty as an Arabian pigeon,' said Fenella approvingly.

'I still can't believe we're about to go back into the past!' said Jess.

Jason nodded. 'And then we've got the jungle in Peru and Mount Quamquangle to look forward to!'

Fenella raised her wings as far as she could in the cramped confines of the kiln and hunted about her sides for a particular feather. 'Now, where is the feather you need . . . Ah, there it is.' She plucked one out with her beak and tossed it to Michael. The feather was grey and barely glimmered in the light. It felt cold to the touch.

'That feather's as old as I am,' Fenella told them. 'One of the first I grew at the time of my last rebirth. It'll take you right back to that August day. The ashes of my nest should still be warm.'

Jason raised his eyebrows. 'You mean we'll arrive right next to the last nest of your old self?'

'Well, to be honest, dearie, I'm not quite sure exactly where you'll end up but you should be there or thereabouts.' Fenella gave a feeble cough. 'The map will guide you in any case.'

'Of course!' said Michael. 'Let's see it, Jase.'

Jason pulled the map from his pocket and Michael, Milly and Jess gathered round to see. It showed what looked to be a complicated zigzagging maze, and a large red cross.

'Funny how these words are still there on the map.' Jason pointed. '*Know Yourself, Trust Yourself, Believe in Yourself.* Skribble said he wanted us to look at them carefully.'

'Oh, yes, Jess told me you'd seen Skribble,' said Fenella. She looked sad. 'I can't think why he didn't pop by and see me.'

'He didn't seem quite himself,' Milly confided.

'These words were written on the paper when you were searching for us, Fenella,' Jason realized. 'They must have been meant for you.'

Fenella gave a brief squawk. 'I don't think so, lovey. I don't *know* myself, 'cause I've no idea why I've laid an egg. And I certainly can't *trust* myself to hang onto my egg after losing the last one.' She shivered and seemed to shrink into herself a little. 'And how can I believe in myself, eh? If I was any kind of useful bird I'd just get on with this business of hatching an egg, wouldn't I? I wouldn't need to faff around with all this improbable paraphernalia.'

'You are a useful bird,' Milly protested.

'Yeah,' Michael put in. 'You're . . .' He shrugged, blushing. 'Well, you're cool.'

'Decidedly chilly, more like!' Fenella smiled at him gratefully. 'But thank you, my pets.' She ruffled her wings. 'Well, I can make a good start on building my nest while you're gone, can't I? Oh, but mind out for Bab Zuweila when you're looking for the ash.'

Michael blinked. 'Babs who?'

'Bab *Zoo-way-la!*' Fenella emphasized each syllable. 'They were just building a big wall around Cairo, that year, and Bab Zuweila's a grand old stone gate on the southern side. It was the perfect spot to watch the sunset. I seem to recall I hung around there for a bit after I was reborn, and it wouldn't do for you to run into my earlier self at that point in time. It wouldn't do at all.'

'We'll be careful,' Jason told her.

Jess took a deep breath and checked her watch. 'We should get going. It's eleven thirty now, so we've got a good while before we need to start worrying about sunset.'

Michael raised the old, cold feather and the others reached out to touch it. 'I guess when we go into the past, we switch the time spell around.'

'You do.' Fenella nodded and coughed again, a hard, hacking sound. 'Just remember what I told you about causing ripples in the birdbath of time,' she added. 'You must pass through the past like shadows.'

'We'll try,' Milly promised.

Michael nodded. 'And wrap up warm or something, Fenella, OK?' He took a deep breath. *'Time of yore, be never gone.* We want August the twenty-sixth, 1092!'

The feather burned copper-bright in his hand, and a strange coldness icicled through his fingers. The world began to spin again. A golden haze settled on the workshop around them, and the ground seemed to lurch as if they'd stepped inside some great celestial lift headed for the ground floor of creation.

'Next stop, the eleventh century.' Jason gasped as reality dissolved around them. 'Here we go!'

Chapter Eleven

Jason felt the gold haze lift and gasped as his senses were assaulted from all sides.

It was burning hot, the sunlight so bright he had to shield his eyes. Smells of spice, sweat and sewage thickened the air. The breeze was like a hairdryer blasting his skin, and he tasted sand on his lips. He and the others had arrived in a crowded, crumbling street of sun-dried brick. Market stalls were arranged in a haphazard jumble, with crowds of customers pushing past the children as if they weren't there. The noise was incredible – cries in exotic accents mingled with the braying of donkeys and the creak of cartwheels. Ornate towers stretched up from sun-baked mosques like tall candles, teetering high above the surrounding buildings.

'Wow!' was all Jason could find to say.

'I can't believe it!' Milly said.

Jess was staring around in amazement. 'We've made it. We've travelled into the past!'

Michael grinned. 'Good to know that the bird's not entirely useless!'

'You don't fool us,' teased Jess. 'You really like Fenella.'

Michael frowned. 'Shut up!' His frown deepened as a large man pushed past him with a camel. 'Maybe we should get out of the way a bit.'

'And keep our voices down.' Jess warned, still clutching the feather as she looked around. 'We don't want everyone knowing we're foreign.'

'Our clothes stand out a mile,' Michael muttered. Most people were wearing long, grimy robes and were walking through the dust barefoot or in sandals. He looked down at his Nikes, and the hems of his jeans sticking out from beneath the nylon trousers, and felt horribly conspicuous. 'Let's keep our heads down and check the map.'

'It's 1092,' Jason breathed, still boggling as Michael led the way across the filthy street to a crumbling wall. Scrawny chickens flapped about their ankles as they walked. 'I just can't believe it.'

Jess laughed out loud. 'We spend years learning history at school and then suddenly we're here, right in it!'

'Just hope I don't lose that feather,' said Michael, 'or we really *will* be right in it!'

'Don't you dare.' Milly warned him.

'As if.' Michael was doing his best to sound laid back, but Jason could see the excitement dancing in his eyes. 'Get the map out then, Jase.'

Jason unrolled the map. The street-lines zigzagging across the parchment seemed deeper and better defined in the scorching sunlight. A red X was pulsing in a strange sort of circle, quite close by. 'That must be where Fenella's nest is! I wonder where she's built it? It looks like it's this way.'

Cautiously, keeping tight hold of the map, Jason set off through the chaotic city streets. Medieval Cairo seemed a place of great contrasts. Small children in rags stared wide-eyed as rich, perfumed ladies swept past. Beggars crowded the gutters, their arms outstretched towards well-to-do men browsing stalls crammed with exotic delicacies.

Michael lingered beside a stall of crockery. 'I bet a couple of these clay plates would be worth a fortune back in our time. Why didn't I bring my phoenix gold?'

Jess frowned, reached through her robes and checked her trouser pocket. 'Actually, I've got one of *my* bits of phoenix gold with me!'

'Lend us some,' Michael urged her.

'No way,' she retorted. 'Let's just find the ashes and go back.'

'I think we've got to go down here,' Jason declared, peering round the corner into a quieter, narrow street.

They set off again. The street backed onto some old ruins, and the houses were made from the same stone.

'We're nearly there.' Jess was peering at the map over Jason's shoulder.

'These ruins look a bit like old-fashioned temples,' said Jason. 'I bet they were still being used when Fenella was reborn before this time, so she came back to the same spot!'

'Look!' Michael stopped in his tracks.

Jason gulped. Three bearded men wearing black and gold robes were climbing over the low roofs of the buildings. They had long swords in both hands. Behind them, ten more men were swarming over the ruins. His heart thumping, Jason looked up from the red cross in its circle on the map to a tall, broken pillar stretching up to the sky like the tusk of a long-dead mammoth, crowned with a crumbling mess of smoking black sticks. 'There it is,' he hissed. 'We've found the nest.'

'But *they've* found it first!' groaned Michael as two of the black-robed men lifted down the large spiky bundle.

Milly pointed. 'Look at the picture on their robes!'

Jason squinted into the sunlight and saw that the stylized figure of a golden bird was embroidered on the garments.

'Fenella said she'd had phoenix-worshipping cults after her,' Jess remembered.

Michael nodded. 'Looks like those men must be in her fan club.'

'What are we going to do?' asked Jason nervously. 'I bet they won't let us get near the ashes.'

'Maybe we could *buy* the ashes from them,' suggested Jess. 'With phoenix gold.' She pulled one of Fenella's glittering gifts from her pocket. 'They're bound to know what it is.'

'Too risky,' Michael began to say, but then Milly grabbed Jess by the arm.

'Oh no!' she said in dismay. 'They've seen it – the gold!'

With a stab of alarm, Jason saw that Milly was right. One of the sword-wielding guards was calling out to his friends behind him, while the other two watched the children intently. Suddenly one of the men cupped a hand to his mouth and gave a strange warbling cry. He started to wave his sword hand at them in a come-here gesture.

Michael gulped. 'He wants us to go over. Quick! Run!'

But as the children turned, they found two more swarthy, bearded men in black and gold blocking their way. 'That guard wasn't calling to us, he was calling to *them*!' Jason cried.

Jess shrieked as one of the men moved in and grabbed her by the wrist, twisting hard. He stared down at the phoenix gold in her hand and started babbling in excitement.

'Get off her!' Michael shouted. Milly kicked the man on the shin but his friend unsheathed his sword and raised it threateningly. Jason glanced behind and saw the men on the rooftops scrambling down to street level, ready to get them.

'The feather!' Michael yanked it from his pocket and held it up in the air. 'Everyone touch the feather, I'll get us out of here.'

'Don't show them that, Michael!' Jason yelled. 'They might recognize it—'

But it was too late. The man with the raised sword gasped at the sight of the feather, his eyes out on stalks. He lunged forward, his large hands closing on it. 'No!' Michael

shouted, tightening his grip. Desperately, he twisted clear . . .

And the feather snapped in half!

Michael stared at the remains of the precious feather in shock, while Milly screamed at the top of her lungs. A few wary faces appeared at the windows of the houses around them to see what all the noise was about. Out of ideas himself, Jason started shouting too. If they could only get someone to help them . . .

But already one of the men was bundling Jess away down the narrow dusty street.

Jason forgot about the feather, 'Get off my sister!' he roared. He stooped to pick up a rock and threw it at the man holding Jess. The shot went wide and he yelled in frustration.

Michael ran after the men, bunching his fists. 'Hang on, Jess!' But the man with the half-feather lashed out with his sword and Michael recoiled. 'Ow!' he shouted, falling to the dusty ground.

'Michael!' cried Jess frantically through a mouthful of fingers.

Milly ran to her brother. He had a long, red cut down his bare forearm. Michael stared at the wound in disbelief. 'He could've taken my arm off – *that's* what my future self tried to warn me about!'

'Guys, look!' Jason pointed at the rest of

the black-and-gold gang. They had scrambled down from the rooftops and were pounding away down the street in the opposite direction. 'We've got to go after Jess!'

Michael nodded, shoved his half-a-feather in his pocket and jumped back up. 'It's three against two – four if Jess can break that bloke's grip.'

'If only they didn't have swords,' Milly wailed.

Jason bit his lip. 'We've got to try. Come on!'

They ran off down the higgledy-piggledy streets in pursuit. But almost straight away, they came to a junction and couldn't tell which way Jess and her abductors had gone.

Milly marched up to the nearest merchant. 'Did you see a girl dragged away by two bad men? Did you see where they went?'

The merchant stared down at her, baffled by her strange language and appearance. Michael grabbed hold of her hand and pulled her to the left. 'We'll try down here,' he announced grimly.

They threaded their way through the busy street. Milly tripped over somebody's foot and Jason nearly lost his turban several times. The street branched off again in three possible directions. Jason chose the middle path, lined on both sides with high turreted towers. But as they turned a sudden corner they found the street completely blocked by a herd of cattle. They tried to turn round and go back, but a crowd had already built up behind them.

Milly looked helplessly at Michael and Jason. 'We've lost them!'

'Wait a minute,' said Michael, turning to Jason. 'The map! It shows where the ashes are, right?'

'Right!' Jason suddenly got his meaning. 'And those men were all dressed the same and looked part of the same group. They went different ways so we couldn't follow them, but they're bound to meet up again later.'

Milly gave a hopeful smile. 'You mean that if we find the ashes on the map, maybe we'll find Jess?'

'And the other half of the feather,' said Michael. 'If we can stick the bits back together, we might just stand a chance of getting out of this place.'

Jason took out the map. The red cross pulsing on the parchment was slowly moving out from the maze of city streets. He felt worried sick. 'I hope Jess is OK.'

Michael winced as he dabbed at his forearm.

'If only we knew a bit more about those weirdo geezers who've taken her . . .'

As he spoke, ornate writing bloomed into being on the map. 'Look!' Jason hissed. 'The map's telling us!'

The Brothers of the Sun Bird
Members of this cult prize phoenix gold above all other things. They believe that the powers of the phoenix can be absorbed by human beings to grant them greatness. Legends handed down by cult members over the centuries claim that if the tip of a phoenix feather is dipped in ink made from the ashes of the great bird's nest, any prophecy then written with that quill-tip will come to pass. One such prophecy states that there will come a child with gold-spun hair who is kin to the phoenix and who may command her to come among men and leave riches.

'They must be bonkers,' said Michael simply.

Milly hugged herself despite the heat. 'And

they've got Jess! They must think she's the girl in the prophecy.'

'Well, we've got to get her back,' said Jason, swallowing hard as the vivid red cross slowed to a halt near the edge of the page. 'The question is – how?'

Chapter Twelve

Numb with fear, thirsty and too shocked even to struggle very hard, Jess found herself manhandled out of the streets and through a valley littered with broken masonry.

Her two captors forced her inside a narrow cave. The sudden cool was welcome, but the inky, frightening blackness was not. With a thrill of foreboding Jess saw flickering light on the rock walls ahead – and next moment found herself shoved forward into the mouth of a large, smoky cavern.

Some kind of underground temple, she realized. It was octagonal in shape and stank of burning tar. Golden Arabic symbols were painted on the eight walls, together with more phoenix designs. Flaming torches hung at intervals against the pitted rock, sixteen in total, all casting an eerie light. A kind of campfire burned in the centre of the cavern, with a small cauldron suspended over it.

Jess started as a man came striding out of the shadows to the rear of the cave. He was dressed in black and gold like those who had brought her here, but even in the flickering firelight she could see his robes were of a finer quality. From the way her captors bowed to him, he was clearly important – a priest, perhaps, Jess thought. He wore a turban set with a large amber jewel in the shape of a phoenix. He marched right up to Jess and peered at her closely with dark, intelligent eyes.

One of her guards held out the phoenix gold he'd taken from her. The priest took it reverently and kissed it.

The other guard held out the half-feather. The priest studied it closely – then gave Jess a gloating smile and spoke a word in his indecipherable language.

'Ow – get off!' Jess cried as her headdress was pulled away to reveal her blonde hair. The priest's smile grew even wider.

There was a scrabbling noise behind her as two more cultists came into the cave, carefully carrying the ashen remains of Fenella's nest between them.

'Ahhhh,' said the priest, smiling as the

newcomers bowed down towards him. The two men then rested the nest carefully on top of the cooking pot. One of them took a torch from the wall and poked it into the centre of the crumbling nest, knocking ash and charcoal down into the tarry substance smoking away inside the cauldron.

Tears prickled in Jess's eyes. 'Fenella needs that ash,' she whispered. She had never felt more scared and helpless in her life.

The priest turned back to Jess with a triumphant look on his face. '*Alchiber,*' he said, and mimed dipping the stem of the broken feather into the cauldron before scrawling in the air.

'Writing?' guessed Jess. 'Ink?'

The priest turned and crossed to the cauldron and reverently scratched the tip of the broken feather against the crumbling outer edge of the nest. Then he raised the feather high into the air, ready to dip it into the tarry concoction bubbling away in the cauldron . . .

'Um . . .' came a familiar voice, 'please may we have our feather back?'

Jess turned and gasped. It was Michael, standing in the doorway to the cavern temple with his hands behind his back.

Where're Jason and Milly? But as the thought

flashed across her mind, the nearest cultist growled and raised his sword.

'Be careful, Michael!' she screamed.

As the man approached, Michael swung out one arm and revealed what he was holding – his Game Boy Advance. At the press of a button, the little screen lit up and showed a scene of a knight fighting a dragon while tinny rock music echoed out around the cave at top volume. The man with the sword backed away in alarm and looked to the priest for guidance.

As he did so, Jess took full advantage of the distraction – she stamped on the foot of one captor and elbowed the other in the stomach. Both were caught off guard, and as they staggered back Jess wrenched her arms free and pointed to the priest. 'He's got it, Michael!'

'Right . . .' Michael held up his Game Boy like a protective shield, swinging it slowly from side to side. The gang cowered as he brought the games system to bear on them.

Of course, Jess realized. *People in this time have never seen anything like a Game Boy!*

'Fear my internal front-light and two-hundred-and-forty by one-hundred-and-sixty pixel resolution!' shouted Michael, trying not to cough on the smoke as he advanced on the astonished priest. 'Bow down before my five-hundred-and-twelve simultaneous colours in character mode! And *give me the other half of my feather!*'

With a sudden movement he swiped the feather from the priest's grip. Jess lunged for her phoenix gold – but the priest yelled out a string of words and held the little slab over his cauldron, clearly threatening to drop it into the evil-smelling mixture unless Michael backed off.

'You can keep the gold,' said Jess, grabbing a handful of crunchy nest ash. 'This is worth a million times more.'

'What?' Michael turned to argue – and glimpsed black-and-gold movement behind her. One of the cultists was lumbering towards them, sword raised. As Michael took in that particular sight, the priest lunged for his Game Boy.

Desperately, Michael ducked out of the way so that the priest and guard collided. At the same moment, Jess gave both cultists an almighty shove that sent them staggering against the cauldron, knocking it flying in a blaze of cinders. Both men howled and hopped about, their bare feet singed by the campfire wood, and other cultists tried to pick up the hot metal container before its contents spilled out completely.

Michael ran for the exit. 'Let's make like bananas – and peel!'

Jess frowned as she raced after him, clutching the ashes. 'You mean "split".'

'Damn!' Michael burst out into the passageway. 'My action hero lines need a bit of work!'

Jess could hear angry voices and footfalls echoing close behind. Michael ran on ahead, the Game Boy's bright screen pushing back the shadows to light their way.

'They're gaining on us!' Jess panted. 'Where's Jason? And Milly?'

'Funny you should ask,' Michael shot back. 'They've got my sash.'

'This is no time to worry about your clothes!' Jess exclaimed, realizing that the blue sash around his waist was missing.

Michael grinned. 'This Sun Bird bunch are the ones who should be worried!' The passage narrowed ahead, with large rocks protruding at ground level either side of the passage. 'When I give the word, keep running but jump in the air.'

'What?' Jess frowned.

'WORD!' Michael yelled, leaping into the blackness. Jess copied him. As she cleared the ground, she glimpsed a length of blue material move beneath her. Looking over her shoulder, she gasped to see Jason and Milly crouched either side of the passage, pulling Michael's missing sash taut between them – a shiny nylon tripwire!

A second later the first cultist ran straight into it at full speed and fell flat on his face. His friends behind him couldn't stop in time and went the same way. Soon several of the Brothers were trapped in a struggling pile, blocking the passageway.

'We did it!' cried Milly, jumping to her feet.

'Did you get the feather?' Jason asked Michael breathlessly.

'Yes! He was brilliant!' Jess beamed as Milly threw her arms around them both. 'And actually, so was I!' She waved her blackened hands, still clutched tightly together. 'I got the ash!'

Milly whooped. 'Fantastic!'

'But the Brothers won't stay down for long,' said Michael. 'Come on!'

He led the charge for the exit. The brightness of the Egyptian daylight broke blindingly around them as they charged away down the rubble-filled valley, Michael in front, Jess clutching the ashes, and Jason and Milly holding hands as they ran.

Michael paused behind a big boulder. 'Right, let's touch the two bits of feather together and whiz ourselves back to the present. Everyone hold on!'

Panting and grimy, the others did so, hearts pounding as they cast nervous glances over their shoulders. 'Say it then, Michael!' Jess urged him.

'*Time before us, take us on,*' he intoned, '*back to the day we left!*'

The children waited tensely. But nothing happened.

'It must be really broken!' said Milly fearfully.

Jess felt as if icy water was filling her stomach. 'We're stuck here in the past.'

'We can't be,' said Michael, uselessly pressing the two parts of the feather together. 'We just can't be!'

'Bab Zuweila,' cried Jason. 'That new gateway Fenella told us about – the perfect place to watch the sunset, she said.'

Michael stared at him incredulously. 'We're up to our ears in dog-doo and you want to watch the *sunset?*'

Jason shook his head. 'Fenella told us to stay away from that gate in case she was hanging around. Perhaps she can help us.'

'But why would she?' Milly said. 'She told us to steer clear of her.'

'It's the Sun Bird Brothers' swords I want to steer clear of!' cried Michael as he saw the cultists burst out of the cave entrance. *'Run!'*

Chapter Thirteen

The Brothers of the Sun Bird chased after the children, dark figures against the bright landscape, drawing closer like swift shadows. Michael's mouth was parched and his arm was still throbbing. He and the others ran back into the bustling city, turning this way and that down the narrow streets until they finally they came up against a dense crowd of people blocking their way like a living wall. Glancing behind them, they saw to their relief that they seemed to have lost their pursuers.

'Rest a sec,' croaked Michael, slumping against a wall.

'Let's check the map,' panted Jason. 'See if we can find Bab Zuweila.'

'Why are those men still chasing us?' Milly gasped.

'They think Jess is the golden-haired girl in the prophecy written in phoenix ash, remember?'

Michael winced as his calves began to cramp. 'They reckon she can talk to the phoenix, command her to weave gold and stuff.'

'What?' Jess looked down at the sweet-smelling charcoal chunks in her hand, appalled. 'The priest said they were making ink, and I saw them add nest ash to the mixture . . .' She swallowed back tears. 'But if they think I'm a girl from a prophecy they'll *never* stop chasing me, wherever we go.'

Jason scanned the parchment. 'I can't see any gates on this map!'

'You don't need to . . .' Milly was looking at the crowd of people in front of them. The Egyptians were chattering and pointing up at a tall stone tower that was built like a miniature castle. She had glimpsed a glint of gold right at the very top. 'I – I think that must be it right in front of us!'

Michael staggered back up and gasped. 'And look, there's Fenella!'

Jess and Jason craned their necks. Sure enough, Michael was right – a squat golden bird was perched right at the top of the tower, staring out at the first pink wisps of sunset.

'But how are we going to speak to her?' said Milly desperately. 'She'll never see us over these crowds.'

'And she wouldn't recognize us even if she did,' Jess pointed out. 'She hasn't met us yet.'

'*Fenella!*' Jason yelled at the top of his lungs, and Milly joined in. A few people glanced back at them with irritated expressions, then returned their gaze to the incredible creature on the gate tower.

Michael sifted through some pebbles in the dusty ground and selected some small ones. Then he started lobbing them up at the tower. 'Oi! Bird!' One pebble struck the tower beside her, but went unnoticed. 'Come on, I just need one clear shot.' Weighing the largest pebble he had left in one hand, he hurled it at the phoenix.

And cracked her right on the head!

'He shoots, he scores!' yelled Michael as the young Fenella squawked and fluttered up into the air.

The phoenix hovered in midair for a few moments, silhouetted against the setting sun, a beautiful, unearthly sight. Then she swooped down towards Michael, talons outstretched!

'Ow!' yelled Michael as she gripped hold of his shoulders and slung him to the dusty ground. 'Get off, you dumb bird!' He tried to push away the furious phoenix. But already the chattering crowd of people were surrounding them. Milly and Jess were knocked over in a flurry of flailing limbs – and as Jess fell, the precious ash was jarred from her hand. 'No!' she yelled, reaching out for it. But in seconds, sandaled feet had trampled it into the dust.

The phoenix rose into the air again, taking off

in a flurry of feathers. The crowd surged after her, back towards the huge arched gateway.

Milly stared up to the pink-hued sky. The golden bird was fast disappearing from sight. 'She's leaving!'

'We blew it.' Jess stared at the dusty ground, but there was no trace of blackness there. 'And I lost the ash.'

Jason gulped suddenly, looking behind her. 'But the Brothers of the Sun have *found* us.'

Jess whirled round to see the priest himself standing at the end of the street, his twenty-strong band of black-and-gold brothers behind him.

'I can't run any more,' groaned Milly. 'I just *can't*.'

'Use your Game Boy, Michael,' Jess urged.

'No time for playing,' Michael told her. 'It's time to fly.' He held up the feather again. 'Everyone grab hold. One last try.'

'But it won't work,' Milly said, in tears. 'We know it doesn't work.'

'It might this time,' said Michael. 'Do it!'

The priest and his Brothers walked menacingly towards them. Jason, Milly and Jess all reached out and held the feather.

'*Time before us, take us on,*' said Michael. 'Back to the day we left!'

A golden light started to spark around Jess's vision. Was it sunstroke or was it . . . ?

'Magic,' she breathed as a familiar weightlessness started to tingle through her body. She saw the band of Sun Bird Brothers gasp and fall to their knees, saw the priest's deep, determined eyes as he broke into a run, reaching out for her . . .

'Too late!' she shouted as with a thrill of exhilaration she felt herself fading away. The priest lunged for her but touched nothing but dust as he fell on his face.

'So long, suckers!' Michael yelled, and Jason and Milly whooped with delight as they too felt themselves spiral away. Jess's final glimpse of Cairo was of the priest, his dark eyes fixed on her, his lips curling in a cruel and knowing smile . . .

The next moment, with a lurch, the four of them found themselves back in Mr Milton's workshop. Through the windows, the sky was tinged red with the coming sunset.

'Just in time,' whispered Jason, as the four of them collapsed in a sweaty heap. 'I've got a can of lemonade in my bag.'

'Gimme,' Michael ordered. Within seconds, the can had been opened, passed round and drained dry.

Suddenly the kiln door was pushed open and a familiar golden beak stuck out. 'You're back!' Fenella said, hopping over to her usual place on the workbench. 'Oh, my little turtle-doves, look at the state of you!'

Milly clambered up and hugged the bird around the neck, but the heat was too much for her and she had to step back. Fenella clucked apologetically. 'Whatever happened, loveys?'

'That's what I want to know,' said Jess, wiping her eyes. 'How did you do it, Michael? How come the feather worked this time?'

'Because this time it *wasn't* broken.' Michael passed her the feather. 'See?'

Jess, Jason and Milly looked down at the old, cold feather. Where it had broken before it was now bound with a glittering skein of gold.

'What's that?' Jess peered at it. 'It's . . . another feather! A tiny one wrapped around it.'

Michael nodded to Fenella. 'She shook a few loose when she was attacking me. The feather was hot and soft, sort of bendy, so I wrapped it round the feather and it just melted into the split. *Fixed* it.'

'Let me see that,' said Fenella. She clumsily pecked the feather out of Jess's palm. 'Goodness, you broke the original! And you patched it up with one of my fledgling feathers. Yes, a young feather can easily jump-start an old one, though you did well to get hold of it . . .' She shook her head. 'Wait a sec, pet – you mean you saw my younger self? You met me as I was a thousand-odd years ago, just reborn?'

'Um, yes,' Jason admitted. 'I know you said we shouldn't. Sorry.'

'Michael hit you on the head with a stone,' said Jess.

'I was only trying to get your attention,' Michael protested.

Fenella frowned. 'That was *you*? You were the little Herbert who conked me on the head when I was trying to commune with the setting sun!' She broke off, coughing.

'But we had to!' Jason stuck up for Michael. 'The Brothers of the Sun Bird were after us and they'd broken the feather—'

'That bunch of fawning upstarts!' Fenella said between coughs. 'Only after my lovely gold. Oh, and ash from my nest for their silly prophecies . . .'

'Ash.' Jess's mouth turned dry. 'Oh, Fenella . . . in all the excitement of coming home, I . . .'

'Yes, lovey?' asked Fenella, looking at her with a hopeful smile. 'You did get some ash, didn't you?'

Jess could feel herself turning red, and saw tears welling up in Milly's eyes.

'Yeah, course we did,' said Michael, reaching into his filthy tunic and pulling out several dark, crumbling lumps. 'Here you go – is it enough?'

'Oh, my sweet little Blue Indian Ring-Neck Parrot!' The sight of the ash seemed to give Fenella a new burst of energy and she gave a jubilant squawk. 'Ooooh, yes! Smell that myrrh! Ash from a phoenix nest is extremely potent, you know. Oh, thank you, thank you – a thousand million times, thank you!' She flapped over to Michael and started pecking him clumsily about the face, causing him to back away.

'Steady!' He grinned. 'I'm still black and blue from when we tangled a thousand years ago!'

Jess stared at Michael as he deposited the ash safely on the workbench and dusted his hands. 'How did you manage to get it?' she hissed.

'The bird had just been reborn, hadn't she?' He smiled. 'She must've been standing in that burned-up nest just a few hours earlier, 'cause her talons had big clods of ash stuck in them. When she attacked me, they came loose.'

'Oh, thank heavens!' Jess grabbed him in a hug. 'And thank *you*, Michael. For coming to get me.'

Michael blushed and looked down. 'Whatever.'

'The best and bravest of all boys!' said Fenella fervently.

Michael hastily backed away before she could start trying to kiss him again.

'Well, I guess we'd better be getting back,' said Jess as Fenella started to peck up the ash and put it in the kiln. 'It's getting dark.'

Milly nodded. 'And these things will have to be washed before I give them back tomorrow.'

Michael stared at them. 'We've just survived the

adventure of a lifetime and you're worried about the washing? We should be out partying!'

'I'm too tired to celebrate,' said Jess. 'And it's school tomorrow.'

'Oh, yeah.' Michael's enthusiasm drained away. 'I've just taken on a load of sword-swinging medieval madmen, but I can't tell my mates that, can I? And they all think my little stepbrother can beat me up.' He looked at the slice on his arm. 'They'll probably say *you* did this!'

'And it's another day closer to exams,' Jess added.

'And I've got my school football challenge on Tuesday.' Jason groaned. '*And* your *Annie* audition is getting closer too, Milly.'

'So it is.' Milly looked down at her grubby trousers and sighed.

Fenella burst out coughing again and they all looked round. She was sitting on the worktop, looking drained.

'Fenella, are you OK?' Milly asked anxiously.

'I've told you, don't go worrying about me, my little finch. I'll be just fine.' Fenella heaved a sigh. 'But oh, you've had such a dreadful time. You've put yourself in such danger for me – and done it twice. I simply can't ask you to do any more. I can't ask you to risk your lives for a phoenix's foolish fancy. I forbid it!'

'No way!' said Michael. 'We've got two things

from your list and we're going to get the rest.' He looked at the others. 'Aren't we?'

Jason, Jess and Milly all nodded firmly.

'Peru and Mount Quamquangle here we come!' said Jess.

'Bless you,' said Fenella fervently. 'Well, whatever, you must come and find me after you've been to school. Have a lovely day.' She took a laboured breath. *''Tis education forms the common mind!* Who said that? That old poet – Alexander Pope! Besotted with me, he was – silly old fool. I had to leave England and spend the rest of the eighteenth century in America.'

'You know so much about history,' said Jason.

Fenella smiled. 'I've lived it, pet. Here, there and yonder. The noble and notable have always had a knack of finding me . . . just look at you four!'

Jess cleared her throat. 'Fenella, that ash we fetched will give your chick experience, right?'

The phoenix nodded. 'So Skribble says, lovey.'

'Would it work on people?' Jess went on. 'Would it make them . . . clever?'

'I suppose it might communicate some of the great wisdom I've gathered over the centuries to those with the right minds . . .' Fenella gathered herself and hopped into the kiln. 'Now, goodnight, my kind, brave ducklings! Goodnight to you all . . .'

'Goodnight,' Jess murmured, lost in thought.

And as the others said their farewells to the phoenix until tomorrow, she picked up the battered old feather from the workbench and studied its blackened tip.

Then she slipped it carefully up her sleeve, waved goodbye to Fenella and left the workshop.

Chapter Fourteen

Jess sighed and stared at her open history book. Now back in her bedroom at Moreways Meet, revising by the light from her desk lamp, while Milly slept peacefully in the bed across the room, she could hardly believe that just a few hours ago she had been caught up in life-threatening danger in Egypt. Already it felt like a fading dream. *But it was real*, she thought, looking at the broken and dusty golden feather on her desk, and at the neat pile of costumes Milly had washed.

With a shiver, she remembered the final look the Sun-Bird priest had given her. Such a knowing look in his dark, watchful eyes . . .

There is always one who watches, Skribble had said.

'That priest is long gone,' she told herself

firmly, and looked again at her history book:

John Hancock (1737–93) was president of the Continental Congress. He used his wealth to help finance the American Revolution.

Jess leaned her forehead on her hand. There was so much to learn. She had history first thing the next morning and her teacher, Mrs Riley, was bound to give them a test. She always did. *I've hardly done any revision, the last few days.* Jess hit her head with her fist. 'Go in, go in, go in,' she muttered to the words on the page.

But they didn't. Instead pictures of the crowded streets in Cairo filled her mind – the clothes people were wearing, the buildings, the sounds and smells. *Pity I'm not doing medieval Egypt in history,* she thought.

Her eyes glanced towards the feather again. *Maybe I could use it to go to America at the time of the Revolution . . .*

She dismissed the idea immediately. Even if the repair held, the feather was probably almost out of time-puff by now.

Jess turned the feather slowly over in her hands, looking at the ashy tip that the priest had made ready to write with. Fenella had said that it could give great wisdom to someone with the right mind . . .

Excitement gathered in the pit of her stomach as she thought of everything Fenella must have seen in the last twenty thousand years. *If I knew all that,* thought Jess, *I'd get straight As in every history test!*

She looked at the ash. She was so tempted. Just one little taste and maybe she could have all Fenella's phoenix wisdom. Fenella said she'd been in America during the eighteenth century. Maybe she knew all about the revolution . . .

Quickly, Jess licked the ash before she could change her mind.

For a split second all she thought was, *Ew, it tastes like grit!* But the next second a bright gold light seemed to explode inside her head. Pictures flashed through her mind, pictures of things Fenella had seen, people she had met – kings, sultans and emperors. There were fields of corn, rivers, mountains, woods, a pyramid with a camel beside it . . . The haze of images continued – fields and forests, castles collapsing, the Eiffel Tower flinging girdered arms up to the sky, two armies fighting on a great muddy plain as she flew overhead.

Jess gasped and covered her eyes with her hands but the pictures crowded into her head, flashing faster and faster – until suddenly, they stopped.

Jess slowly lowered her hands. Milly shifted slightly in her bed. The streetlights were shining in through a gap in the curtain.

OK, I'm still here. I'm all right, thought Jess with a feeling of relief.

She shook her head slightly. It felt strange. Almost as if her mind went on and on, much deeper and much further than it had before.

Her eyes fell on the open book in front of her. As she looked at the picture of John Hancock – a tall man with a long nose, wearing a grey wig and a smart jacket with gold trim – a commentary seemed to start up in her head. *Ooooh, that John Hancock, now he was a nice man . . .* It sounded like Fenella, somehow speaking inside her mind! *Got me out of a tight spot with an over-curious raccoon. Everyone thought he had got his money from a smuggling uncle but little did they know about the phoenix gold that I gave him. I stayed with him quite a while. The times we sat in his study as he practised his signature for that Declaration of Independence document he was all in tizz about. Lovely, he was, proper lovely . . .*

Jess caught her breath. This was seriously weird! She felt like she really knew John Hancock, just as Fenella had once done. *I bet I'll be able to answer any questions Mrs*

Riley asks about him, she thought in delight. She turned over the next page of her history book and read the title: 'The Battle of Bunker Hill.'

Oh dearie me, what a to-do there was about that! Fenella's voice seemed to say. *There I was, nesting quietly in a chestnut tree on a lovely sunny night in June and suddenly all these soldiers arrived, about to have a battle. Of course when they spotted me, their leader, dear William Prescott, immediately paid me the full respect and reverence due to a phoenix and moved all those men to a different hill two thousand feet away. Bless them. The fighting that went on though! Gave me quite a turn!*

Jess broke off her thoughts, and the phoenix voice fell obligingly silent. 'Amazing,' Jess breathed. But her history exam wasn't just going to be about things that Fenella might have seen or people she had met. There were often questions about long boring negotiations and treaties. How would the phoenix know about those?

Once again, it was almost as if she had Fenella in her head, tossing helpful memories her way. *Well, I remember sitting with that fine, upstanding man, Benjamin Franklin, in 1783, talking about the Treaty of Paris and how he and his friends were about to sign it to end the war. I reminded him to make sure they could do their fishing up in Newfoundland. You can't beat a bit of cod from the seas around there. I do like a nice bit of fish now and then . . .*

A grin spread across Jess's face.

'Brilliant,' she whispered.

'Bye, then,' Jess called to Jason and Milly, picking up her school bag and heading out of the kitchen. She hadn't had a chance to tell them what she'd done the night before, but they were bound to think it was a good idea.

Oooh, I remember talking about ideas with Marcel Proust, the famous writer, over cakes in 1919. I've no idea what he was on about. Silly old duffer . . .

Jess shook her head a little worriedly, and the phoenix voice went quiet. As she opened the front door, Michael came hurtling down the stairs, hair flattened with some water, his tie even more crooked than normal. 'Wait, Jess! I'm coming with you!'

Jess blinked. Michael never walked into school with her. He always arrived at the very last second before the bell for registration went, whereas she liked getting in early so she could get herself organized for the day and chat to her friends.

'What's going on?' Jess said as they headed down the drive.

Michael shrugged. 'Just thought I'd walk in with you. Keep you company.'

Jess didn't believe him for a second. 'Is this because you hope your friends will go easier on you after your multiplex disaster on Saturday night if someone else is with you?'

'No!' Michael started to protest. Then he looked away. 'Well . . .'

Jess didn't say anything. She knew she'd feel the same if it was her. They walked along in silence for a few minutes, then Jess decided to confide in him.

'Michael, I . . . I used a bit of magic last night. I tasted some of the ash that was left on the feather.'

'What, you? Little Miss Sensible?' Michael's eyes widened. 'But if it works on you like it's meant to work on the chick, you should be super-brainy by now!' He peered at her. 'You seem normal.'

'I *am* still normal,' said Jess. 'It just seems to have given me some of Fenella's experiences. I know loads about what happened back in the past.' She told him about some of the things she had seen in her mind.

'That sounds cool,' said Michael, looking

impressed. 'You'll have no problem in history now!'

Jess grinned. 'Here's hoping. And, I mean, it's not really cheating, is it?'

'Er, yes. Big time.' Michael shrugged. 'What else would you call it?'

'A helping hand from a friend,' Jess decided, and told herself that was OK.

They reached the school gates and Michael's attention was distracted by his mates – and Rick the Slick – standing round near the bike sheds. They nudged each other as they saw him.

'Hey, Michael!' said Thomas with a grin. 'No one from the primary school mugged you on the way in then?'

'See you brought your big sister as a bodyguard.' Josh smiled at Jess. 'You know, I wouldn't mind a bodyguard if I could find one as fit as that.'

'Nothing about your body's worth guarding,' Jess retorted. 'Catch you later, Michael.' She started to walk away as the sniggering and comments continued behind her.

'No little old ladies jumping out from behind bushes to get you then?' Sam teased.

'There was one,' Michael answered breezily.

'Luckily her Zimmer frame got stuck in a crack on the pavement, so I escaped.'

His mates laughed, and Jess felt a slight wave of relief. Maybe Michael was going to survive the day. *Hope I do too*, she thought as she went into the main block and the double doors swung shut behind her.

Chapter Fifteen

History was Jess's first lesson. 'I am so dreading this exam,' said Colette as they found a table. Jodie and Natasha, their other two friends, had already got their books out behind them. 'Did you get loads of revision done over the weekend?'

'A bit,' said Jess. Then she realized that she couldn't explain her sudden leap in knowledge unless she had been doing some work. 'Well, quite a lot actually. I . . . um, found a good study program on the Internet so I've been working through that.'

'Cool!' said Colette. 'I wish the exams were over. So boring! I've been going over and over the American Revolution all half term.'

Just then, Mrs Riley arrived. She was a young teacher with cropped blonde hair. 'That's what I like to hear, Colette!' she said brightly as she put her books down on her desk. 'In that case you should have no problem with the little test we're going to do this morning!'

There were groans around the class.

'Come on, now! All books shut.' Mrs Riley clapped her hands. 'You're in two teams – let's split you down the middle.' She drew an imaginary line dividing the class in two. 'Team A,' she said, pointing to Jess's side of the room. 'And Team B. First person with their hand up gets to answer the question. If you get it wrong it goes to the other team.'

For once Jess's heart didn't sink. In fact, she felt a growing buzz of excitement. Maybe for once she'd be able to impress Mrs Riley with her knowledge. *I've certainly got some impressing to do,* she thought, remembering the bad grades she'd been getting lately. To be able to take history next year she not only had to do well in the exam but she also had to get a good report from Mrs Riley.

'First question then,' said Mrs Riley. 'What is John Hancock best remembered for?'

Jess's heart leaped. Her hand went up.

Mrs Riley smiled at her. 'Yes, Jessica?'

'For his signature on the Declaration of Independence.'

'Good,' said Mrs Riley, putting a mark on the board for Team A. 'Question two: what were the conditions like at Valley Forge?'

Jess's hand shot up again as she immediately seemed to hear Fenella trilling: *Valley Forge. Oooh, yes. Ever so hot, that was. I had a lovely time there toasting my toes. A little place tucked away behind a stables. Perfect place for a phoenix.*

Everyone else seemed to be suffering from Monday morning exhaustion. 'I think you were first again, Jessica,' said Mrs Riley, with a smile.

'It was very hot at Valley Forge,' said Jess confidently, picturing a small building in her mind. She could almost feel the heat on her skin. 'Boiling. There was a big fire for heating horseshoes and only two small windows.'

Mrs Riley started to frown. 'Whatever do you mean, Jessica?'

'Windows in the forge,' Jess replied. 'In the building.'

A few people giggled.

'Valley Forge is the name of the place where George Washington camped with his army, northwest of Philadelphia,' said Mrs Riley sternly. 'You should know it's not a blacksmith's forge, we only did it the week before half term.'

'Oh, yeah.' Jess felt her cheeks burn. *Fenella must have been at a* different *Valley Forge.*

'Anyone else?' Mrs Riley said.

Colette put up her hand. 'The conditions there were mild apart from over Christmas,' she

166

said when Mrs Riley nodded at her. 'But lots of soldiers died because of bad site management.'

'Good.' Mrs Riley put another mark on the board. 'Now, who can tell me how Mary Hays McCauly got her nickname of Molly Pitcher?'

Oooh, that Mary. A proper nice woman she was. We used to call her Molly Pitcher because she used to bring water out for us birds when she . . .

Jess put her hand up. Mrs Riley nodded at her. 'She was known as Molly Pitcher because she used to put out water for all the birds.'

Mrs Riley stared. 'Water for the birds?'

There were more than just a few giggles this time.

'Miss, miss!' Andrew had his hand up.

'Yes, Andrew?'

'It was because she carried pitchers of water to her husband and his gun crew in battle!'

'That's right. Well done.'

Jess sat quietly through a few questions, not trusting herself to speak, trying to get her thoughts together. But then Mrs Riley asked a question she just had to answer: 'Why did the Battle of Bunker Hill actually take place on Breed Hill?'

Jess raised her arm and earned a stern look from Mrs Riley. 'I'm almost afraid to ask . . .'

'Because the soldiers found a—' Jess caught herself just in time. *Because the soldiers found a very stylish phoenix up in a tree*, she'd been going to say. Mrs Riley would think she was cracking up. 'Because . . . because . . .' She suddenly wondered what reason had been given in the history books. She was sure she had known once but it had gone completely out of her mind.

'Um . . . because they found a rare bird there?' Jess cringed as she said it.

Mrs Riley's eyes almost popped out of her head. 'Intelligent girls should know when to stop clowning and start taking their studies seriously – *if* they want to pass their exams!'

Jess sank down in her seat and saw Colette glance at her in a worried way.

'The soldiers were sent out to fortify Bunker Hill,' drawled Daniel, a boy from the other team. 'Some say they chose Breed Hill at the last minute as it was closer to Boston and so more defensible, others say it was a mistake. No one really knows for certain.'

Mrs Riley smiled and added a point to Team B's score.

'Are you OK, Jess?' Colette whispered.

Jess nodded miserably. But she wasn't. She felt so muddled up. The things she had learned from actual books all seemed to have been pushed right to the back of her head by Fenella's memories and she found herself doubting every answer she wanted to give.

She was very glad when the test was over. But then they started looking through their history books at the Battle of Monmouth and a familiar voice in her head piped up again, saying: *Ooooh no, it didn't happen like that. I remember flying overhead and . . .* It was hard to concentrate with someone else's memories crowding in on her own, and she got told off three times for fidgeting and sighing.

Afterwards, Mrs Riley kept her back at the end of the class and spoke to her seriously. 'Jessica, you're a bright girl. But if you want to have a chance of taking history next year, you need to really knuckle down and revise properly. Do you understand?'

'Yes, miss,' Jess mumbled. She felt awful as she left the classroom.

Colette was waiting for her outside with a sympathetic look. 'I'd forget about that Internet study program if I were you,' she said softly. 'It doesn't seem to have helped you much.'

'No,' Jess sighed. 'It hasn't helped at all.'

Through the rest of the day she found it hard not to mess up. In geography she almost called the river Thames the Winding Grey Ribbon. In science she had to bite her tongue to keep quiet about extra elements she felt should be recorded in the periodic table. And in religious studies she had to try very hard not to blurt out that seven thousand years ago the phoenix was worshipped in ancient China, and start quoting all sorts of strange things about the Spirit of the Fire Mountain.

By home time she was exhausted. She saw Michael walking up the road just in front of her and hurried to catch up with him.

'Hi,' she said. 'How come you're not walking with the others? I thought you'd be fine with them by now.'

Michael pulled a face. 'For five minutes they might forget about Saturday night, but then someone comes out with a smart comment and suddenly they're all laughing again.' He looked totally fed up. 'Just felt like walking home on my own. Wish I'd never thought about using that phoenix gold.' He sighed. 'How about you then? Did the ash help?'

'Oh yes,' Jess said dryly. 'It helped me look like a total idiot. Fenella knows loads of stuff, but not much of it's on the National Curriculum.' She groaned as she remembered the history lesson. 'It was awful, Michael.'

Michael rubbed the scar on his arm from

the day before. 'We were better off without magic in our lives. Magic sucks.'

'Maybe it's what we try to do with it that sucks,' Jess pointed out. 'You didn't need to treat your mates, you're really popular anyway.' She looked at him almost enviously. 'You always have been. So what if Rick's come along? Your friends will still like you because you make them laugh and stuff. Only because they're as stupid as you,' she added, not wanting to sound too soppy.

'You can talk,' Michael countered. 'You don't think it was dumb to eat the phoenix ash? You didn't need to. You've never failed an exam in your life.'

'There's always a first time!' Jess argued. 'Everyone says these exams are harder. And if I do fail them then I won't be able to take the subjects I want next year with all the others.'

'But you've been revising,' Michael told her. 'If you'd just carried on doing that a bit more, I bet you'd pass just fine.'

Jess hated to admit it but a tiny voice at the back of her mind was nagging at her that he might be right.

They trudged on up the hill.

After a few moments, Jess glanced round to see if any of her friends were nearby. They had been really nice to her all day, clearly worrying about her odd behaviour and talking about her exam stress. There was no sign of them but something made her frown. As she turned round, she glimpsed someone ducking furtively behind a tree. She carried on walking but then couldn't resist glancing round again.

This time she saw the person dive behind a lamppost. It was too thin to hide him and she could see his raincoat and most of his body. It was a man with untidy grey hair.

'What's up?' Michael asked.

'Some weirdo is trying to hide from us, I think,' Jess whispered. 'A man.'

Michael looked round himself. 'It's him!' he burst out. He started to hurry on up the hill.

'Who?' Jess said, half running to keep up with him.

Michael lowered his voice. 'I didn't want to say anything before 'cause I didn't want to start a scare. But I saw that guy at the junk shop when I was trying to flog the gold to Barry. He was watching me then, really staring. It reminded me of when we were being spied on by the genies.'

Jess gasped. 'Skribble said to be careful of someone watching us. It must be him.'

'He could be trying to find where we live,' said Michael. 'Let's try and lose him. If we go down Turner's Avenue, we can cut through the playground and then through the field and over the fence into the back garden.

Jess nodded. 'Come on!'

They both sprinted away, their bags bumping against their backs. As they tore across the playground, Jess glanced back. But there was no sign of the man with the grey hair.

They threw themselves over the fence and tumbled in through the back door. Jason and Milly were inside eating chocolate fingers.

'What are you two doing?' Milly said in astonishment as Jess and Michael dumped their bags thankfully on the floor. 'We've just taken the clothes back to the hall.'

'Great,' snapped Michael. He went to the window and checked the garden.

'What's going on?' Jason asked in alarm.

'Are Mum and Mark back?' said Jess in a low voice.

'No,' said Milly.

Jess sighed and shut the door. 'There was this man . . . following us.'

'I saw him in the junk shop on Saturday,' Michael put in quickly; 'tall with thick grey hair and dark eyes.'

Jason gasped. 'Sounds like the man I saw in Quilborough!'

'I forgot you saw someone too,' Michael admitted. 'Well, don't freak, you two, but I think he could be the bloke Skribble was warning us about.'

Milly shivered and looked at Jason. 'What if he's out there waiting for us now? We've got to go to the workshop and see Fenella.'

'And go to the rainforest in Peru and get the herb,' Jason said. 'The one that gives agility and balance.' He sighed longingly. 'I could really use some agility for this football thing at school tomorrow afternoon.'

'No,' Jess said, fixing him with a big-sister look. 'Don't you get any ideas about using that herb. It isn't a good plan, Jason.'

It was clear from the looks he and Milly exchanged that they had been talking about it. 'Why not?' Jason argued. 'Magic could help me.'

'Let's just get the herb and give it to Fenella. I don't think that man tried to follow us. If we all stay together we'll be just fine.' Jess frowned. 'But first, we'd better get changed. We can't turn up in the jungle in our school uniform.'

'Sounds like you're speaking from experience,' said Michael lightly. 'Your own or someone else's?'

Jess glared at him. He winked and sauntered off upstairs.

As she followed him, Jess tried not to think

about the strange man. Instead she focused on the adventure ahead. *Picking a herb can't be that difficult*, she decided. *Least there won't be any mad phoenix priests running about or future selves to avoid. We'll go there and get back in no time. Simple.*

But then Fenella's voice started up in her head. *Oooh, the taste of silphium. It's such a treat – but my, oh my, the price of it if you were to buy it in the market place. Everyone wanted it and there was never enough to go round. I remember—*

'Well I don't want to!' Jess said out loud, and holding her temples she forced the cheery voice into silence. She groaned to herself. Oh, why had she tasted the ash? Why?

Chapter Sixteen

'What are you wearing?' Michael said as he and Jess came back downstairs.

Milly and Jason had put on their long waterproof school coats over their jeans and T-shirts and were wearing their wellies.

'We're going to a rainforest,' Jason said. 'It's going to be really wet!'

'Yeah, you'd better put waterproof things on too,' Milly told the older two.

'Oh, no.' Jess shook her head. 'Imagine if Colette or someone saw me on the way to Mr Milton's!' She winced at the thought.

'I'm with you, Jess,' said Michael. 'No way am I giving Rick the Slick another reason for laughing at me!'

Milly sighed theatrically. 'You'll be sorry.'

Jason followed her out, keeping his eyes peeled for the weird stranger.

'What have you got in there, Jase?' Michael asked, patting a rucksack on Jason's back.

'Supplies,' replied Jason proudly. 'Milly and I were looking at rainforests on the Internet and we've packed insect repellent, a torch, a penknife, first aid kit, some water and—'

Michael rolled his eyes. 'This isn't some sort of wave-your-woggle-around scout camping trip!' he interrupted. 'We're only going to pick some boring old herb and come back.'

'I've decided it's always best to be prepared,' argued Jason. 'We weren't very prepared in Egypt, were we?'

Milly nodded. 'I'm bringing some of my phoenix gold too.' She pulled it out of the pockets of her waterproof coat.

'Milly, we're going to the jungle,' Jess said. 'What use is gold going to be?'

'You never know, there might be some native people there or something,' Milly argued. 'It might come in useful for trading or something.'

'So it's the jungle, here we come!' said Michael as they walked down the drive and turned into the road towards Mr Milton's house.

'I can't wait!' said Milly. 'I hope we see loads of animals. There are lots of them in the rainforest – monkeys and big cats, snakes and spectacled bears—'

'Ssh!' Jess said quickly as she noticed Mr Milton in the garden ahead of them. He was carefully pruning some white roses that grew near the statue of the beautiful lady.

Michael groaned. 'Here's Mr Freaky.'

Milly elbowed him just as Mr Milton looked round. 'Back again? My word, you *are* keen!'

Milly gave him her most innocent smile. 'Oh yes, we love making pots, Mr Milton!'

Jess nodded. 'Thank you so much for letting us use the workshop.'

A pleased expression crossed the old man's face. 'My pleasure. Now don't stop on my account. I'm sure you've got lots to be getting on with and the last thing you want to do is waste time talking to me. Run along, do.'

They said goodbye and hurried to the workshop.

'He's so nice,' said Milly in a low voice. 'I feel a bit mean about tricking him.'

Jess nodded. 'I hope Fenella does give him some gold.'

'I still say he's a weirdo,' said Michael as they opened the door.

The phoenix was moving around behind the kiln. She looked up as they entered. 'Hello, my little chickabiddies.' She jumped out – or tried to. Her first jump didn't work and she had to flap her wings and try again. She landed on the workbench, breathing heavily. Milly noticed her eyes seemed to be slightly glazed over and her feathers seemed to be hanging limply, a few of them falling out to litter the worktop. 'So, you're all ready for your next adventure then?' Fenella paused to take a wheezing breath. 'Off to Peru to get some silphium! Well, well, well.' She coughed hard.

'Oh, Fenella. You really don't look well,' Milly said.

'Bless you, lovey. I'm holding up. Not too long to go now.' Fenella searched through the feathers on her left wing. 'Now, here's the feather you'll be needing.' She plucked it out and offered it to them. It glowed a soft deep gold. 'You'll need to travel back about five hundred years. Silphium became very rare many centuries ago but there were still some clumps dotted here and there for a few hundred years. I spotted one while stopping briefly in the rainforest in Peru in the early fifteenth century. When was it? About 1410?' She tapped her head with one wing. 'Anyway, that feather should guide you.'

Jason carefully took the feather. 'Thank you.'

'Only watch out. The Peruvian jungles are not very safe, not very safe at all.' The phoenix looked worried. 'I really wish you didn't have to go.'

'We'll be fine,' Jess reassured her.

'Yeah, we're just going to zoom there and come straight back,' said Michael. 'Chill out. Um, warm up, I mean. Whatever.'

They all took tight hold of the feather.

'I hope he'll look after you,' mumbled Fenella. 'If he's there.'

'Who?' Milly asked curiously, but before Fenella could answer, Jason was already saying the words:

'Time of yore, be never gone,' he exclaimed. 'Take us to about 1410!'

The four children felt the now-familiar rushing, swirling sensation. They spun round and round in a haze of light. Even before their feet thumped into soggy ground, they felt a hot, wet blanket of heat envelope them and heard the buzz of insects and the squawking, shrieking cries of birds above them.

Milly instantly forgot all about Fenella's last words to them as she opened her eyes. Everything seemed green. Trees towered up into the skies, water dripping off their leaves. Long creepers hung down from the branches and the ground was covered with thick ferns and fallen branches covered with moss.

'Unbelievable!' breathed Jess.

An enormous blue butterfly fluttered in front of Milly's face. In the canopy of branches she could see glimpses of red, green and blue birds. Frogs croaked and insects buzzed all around her. 'Isn't it amazing?' she gasped.

'Ow!' exclaimed Michael as a mosquito landed on his arm. 'I've been bitten! Or stung! Ow!'

'Look at the toucan up there,' Jason said to Milly, pointing into the trees. 'And the macaws.'

'Argh!' yelled Michael as an ant the size of a paperclip tumbled off a nearby leaf and landed on him. He shook it off and another mosquito bit him. 'Yow!' he yelled, slapping at it with his hand. 'We should have got injections from the doctor before we came! Where's that insect repellent, Jason?'

Jason took the can out of his bag but Milly grabbed it off him. 'Thought you said we wouldn't need it,' she teased, holding it just out of Michael's reach.

'Gimme!' Michael lunged for the can of spray but Milly jumped back and, caught off balance, Michael stumbled and fell into a patch of ferns.

Milly giggled but then took pity on him. 'Here,' she said, offering the can of spray, but as he took it a massive black scorpion scuttled out of the bushes at her feet, its hard back wet and shining, its stinging tail curving over its shell. Milly screamed and jumped into the air. Michael yelled and threw himself backwards. Jason shouted and leaped on to a tree stump. Only Jess didn't shout or yell. A voice was speaking in her head.

Oh those pesky scorpions. No respect for a phoenix. Sting you soon as look at you they would. But it's only the ones with a red spot on their back you have to worry about. It'd be curtains for you in less than a minute if one of those got you, but the others, well, they're not so bad.

'It's OK,' Jess shouted happily above the uproar as the scorpion scuttled round in a circle. 'Fenella knows about scorpions. This one won't kill you.'

'Oh whoop-de-do!' Michael scrambled to his feet and joined Jason on the tree stump. 'Perhaps it'll just paralyse us and leave us in intense pain for ever. She only knows about how they affect *her*, remember!'

Jess realized he had a point and hauled Milly out of the scorpion's way. Michael chucked the can of insect repellent at it and it scuttled off. He jumped off the log to pick up the can

– and a stick came hurtling down from the trees and hit his shoulder. 'Ow!' he said, looking up as a chattering, squeaking noise filled the air.

'It's monkeys!' cried Milly in delight as a troop of about twelve monkeys swung through the trees, some of them with babies on their backs. The ones without babies broke sticks off and chucked them down at the children.

Jason ducked, a stick just missing his head. 'They're capuchin monkeys,' he said. 'Do you remember we read about them on the computer, Milly?'

'I don't care if they're *cappuccino* monkeys handing round free samples,' said Michael, shielding his head. 'Let's just get out of here!'

They hurried away through the trees, leaving the shrieking monkeys behind. They had to scramble through ferns and soon Jess and Michael's jeans and T-shirts were soaked through with water from the leaves. Milly and Jason weren't faring much better. It was boiling with their macs on and they were soaked with sweat. They reached a small clearing and stopped, panting for breath.

'Get the map out, Jason,' said Jess, spraying insect repellent all over herself and Milly.

Jason pulled the map out of his bag and unfolded it. It showed a forest of trees with a river running through. A red circle in the bottom left-hand corner marked the children's position. On the bank of the river there was a craggy cliff and a waterfall. Near the bottom of the waterfall, beside the river, was a big red cross.

'Well, that seems clear enough,' said Jess, peering over Jason's shoulder.

'We need to head north-east,' Jason agreed, and pulled a compass out of a small pocket in his bag. 'That way.'

Michael grinned at him. 'OK, sometimes it's good to be prepared! Not cool, but good.'

'Let's go,' begged Milly, pushing her damp hair back from her forehead. She was beginning to feel like she just wanted to grab the herb and go home.

They set off through the dark, fetid forest. They had to scramble and climb over fallen logs, crash through creepers and clouds of insects, trying to ignore the strange rustlings in the bushes around them.

'I think the river must be just through those trees ahead,' Jason said. 'I'm sure I can hear water flowing.'

'And this looks more like a path,' said Michael.

'Maybe the animals come this way to reach the water,' Milly suggested.

Jess nodded distractedly. It was hard to concentrate with Fenella's voice nattering away in her head. *Oooh, there's a red-winged beetle, very tasty. Always crunch nicely in the beak, they do. And some giant ants. You can't beat a mouthful of them when you're in the mood . . .*

The ferns were definitely flattened down now and it was easier to move through the creepers and tree trunks.

'Come on,' said Michael, speeding up, but just as he did so a large animal dropped down from the trees and landed lithely on the path in front of him. He froze. The creature was about two metres long, with a strong muscular body covered with golden brown hair, and cold hazel eyes.

'It's a cougar!' gasped Jason as they all stopped dead. 'A mountain lion!'

The large cat lowered its head and flattened its ears. The bottom of its tail flicked slowly from side to side and a low, savage growl escaped from its mouth.

Michael stepped protectively in front of Milly. Jess grabbed Jason's hand. The icy fear flooding through her had even made Fenella's voice disappear. Every bit of her brain, every scrap of attention was focused on the cougar in front of them.

'What are we going to do?' whispered Milly.

'The feather,' hissed Michael. 'It's our only chance.'

But as Jason fumbled for the feather in his pocket, the cougar crouched its muscular body lower and prepared to spring . . .

Chapter Seventeen

We're gonna die, thought Michael. *Lunch for a giant cat from five hundred years back. And no one will ever know what happened to us . . .* He could feel Milly hanging onto his shoulder, hear Jess's short panicky breaths and Jason still rummaging. The cougar's ears flicked . . .

And then suddenly an ear-splitting bird-like shriek tore through the air. It was so loud the leaves on the trees trembled. The cougar shrank closer to the ground in fear.

There was another deafening cry. *What was it?* Michael felt like his heart was about to burst from his body. Needles of fear pricked every inch of his skin.

The cougar turned and leaped into the bushes.

'It's gone!' gasped Jess.

'Something scared it off,' hissed Michael. 'But what—?'

Then another animal, even larger than the cougar, clattered through the dense canopy of green and bounded up to the children.

Milly screamed, but Michael just stared. This thing was like no animal he had ever seen before. It was as large as a hatchback. It had the body and hind legs of a full-grown male lion and the head, neck and front legs of an eagle-like bird. Its beak was sharp and curved, and its talons even longer. Dark grey eyes glared at them from under feathered brows.

'It's . . . it's a gryphon!' stammered Jess. 'Like Mr Milton's statue.'

The gryphon glared and opened his beak. 'Confounded humans, coming here and making a row, giving me a headache. I could murder the lot of you!' He shook his head crossly. 'Oh well, come on. Let's have your offering.'

He charged forward with an incredible burst of speed and swiped out with one of his taloned, feathered front legs at Milly. She screamed again and there was a dreadful ripping sound . . .

'Milly!' Michael, Jess and Jason all yelled.

Michael expected to see his sister with a massive gash down her body – but only the pocket of her waterproof coat was ripped. The piece of phoenix gold she had brought with her tumbled out and the gryphon caught it neatly in his taloned foot.

'Thank you.' He looked at it and a faint expression of surprise came into his eyes and he nodded approvingly. 'Phoenix gold! Well, well, well, that doesn't come along every day. Such memories I have of phoenix gold . . .' He suddenly tucked it into the feathers on his shoulder, shook off his reflective mood and scowled again. 'Honestly, screaming and creating like hooligans. When I was a young gryphon we were treated with respect, freely offered gold to win our favour. None of this yelling and keeping your gold in your pocket.' He frowned at them. 'Haven't seen any people for a while.' He peered at their clothes. 'My, my, fashions *have* changed!'

'Gryphons! You . . . you love gold,' said Jess in a slow, trembling voice as she heard Fenella talking about the fabled creatures in her head. 'You guarded the old gold mines of Scythia and attacked anyone who came near—'

'Attack!' the gryphon exploded. 'Foolish child, I'd hardly call that an attack! What was I supposed to do, hmm? You weren't exactly standing there offering the gold to me. I had to take it somehow.'

'So . . . so you don't want to eat us?' stammered Milly.

The gryphon looked revolted. 'Eat you? Why in the name of Apollo would I want to do that? You'd taste horrible! Big bones, all that fur on your head . . . ugh! No, give me a rattlesnake or a juicy fruit-bat any day!' He rolled his eyes. 'Don't you get any kind of education these days?'

'Well, they don't exactly teach us about gryphons at school,' said Jason, looking in awe at the amazing creature. 'If anything, they tell us you're . . .' He hesitated. 'Kind of not real.'

'*Not real!*' The gryphon looked apoplectic. 'Don't you think I would know if I wasn't real, boy?' He approached to within an inch of Michael and stared haughtily down his beak at him. 'Now, you've given me your gold, so I'll let you live. Go away and get dressed properly, you annoying children.'

Milly bit her lip. 'Would you mind if we stayed, um, sir? It's just we're trying to find something. A herb. It's called silphium and—'

'Oh, no!' The gryphon shook his head. 'Gold or no gold, you're not having any of the silphium. There are only two clumps left in the world and I'm guarding this one.'

'*You're* guarding it?' echoed Jason, his heart sinking.

'What's so surprising about that?' The gryphon scowled at him. 'My kind make very good guards. We love all nature and we hate things becoming extinct. So yes, I'm guarding this clump, and my cousin Harold is guarding one somewhere in Macedonia.'

Michael frowned. 'Harold the gryphon?'

'Maybe it's a sort of magic translation of his real name,' Jason whispered.

'I guess it's no stranger than a phoenix called Fenella,' muttered Jess.

'So! Not a leaf of silphium shall be taken.' The gryphon flexed one of his large taloned feet warningly and fixed Jason with a fierce look. '*Ever*.'

'But we really need some,' said Michael. 'Not much, just a stalk.'

'Nope.' The gryphon shook his head and raised his talons threateningly. 'Now, shove off!'

The children retreated slightly. 'What are we going to do?' Jess said in a low voice.

'Wee ourselves?' Michael suggested.

'Maybe we should try and make friends,' said Milly. She took a hesitant step towards the gryphon. 'I'm sorry if you think we're rude. My name's Milly. What's yours?'

'My name?' The gryphon's frown softened slightly. 'You know, no human has ever asked me that before. Too busy fussing and bothering about with their own business to remember basic manners.' He coughed. 'As it happens, my name's George.'

Jess, Michael and Jason exchanged looks.

'George!' Milly blinked. 'That's nice. George the gryphon . . .'

'Fenella knew him!' Jess whispered suddenly. 'She told us so, remember? Back when we first went to Mr Milton's house and saw the statue of the gryphons there.'

'You're right,' Milly remembered. 'She said he was grumpy!'

'Shhh.' Jess held a finger to her mouth, trying to blot out the sonic mayhem of the rainforest to hear Fenella's memories murmur in her head. *I always did have a soft spot for George. A bit of a grouch, but then which gryphon isn't? It's not easy being two animals in one and having to wait around for people to bring you gold. I remember us having a lovely time in his eyrie in the Cipo mountains in Brazil before he took himself off to the Peruvian rainforest. Such a sense of duty! But that's no place for a bird like me.*

She caught her breath and looked at George the gryphon. 'You know Fenella, don't you?'

'Fenella?' George looked astonished. 'The . . . the phoenix?'

'Yes,' said Jess quickly. 'She's a friend of yours, isn't she?'

'She was once.' The gryphon's voice softened. 'Ah. I miss our talks but they had to stop when I moved here. The rainforest is no place for a fire bird to live.'

'Fenella's the person we want to help!' Jess burst out. 'That's why we're here.'

'Oh?' George looked interested.

'Yes!' Jason held up the golden feather. 'She's laid an egg and needs some silphium to hatch it.'

The new warmth in George's eyes vanished. 'What do you know about her egg? It was taken from her!' His eyes narrowed. 'Or perhaps you had a hand in the taking. It seems you took her gold, after all!'

'That's not true,' Milly protested. 'She sent us to find the silphium for her hatchling—'

'But her egg was stolen!' said George.

'No she's laid another,' said Milly. 'And she needs four things to help it hatch. One of them is some silphium and . . .'

'Do you think I'm stupid?' The gryphon interupted, 'If a female gryphon can hatch an egg of blue agate without assistance, why should the magnificent phoenix need silphium? You don't know her at all.' The gryphon's voice rose to an angry shriek. 'You've hurt her, haven't you! Hurt her and robbed her. Oh, you've made me angry now.' He reared up, his talons slashing the air, and Michael, Milly and Jason threw themselves aside.

'Remember the sunset over Lagoa Santa!' Jess blurted out.

George hesitated and swung round to stare at her, the anger still blazing in his eyes. 'What?'

'The sunset . . . when you picked the finest cranberry gourd for Fenella . . .' Jess gulped. 'She – she wishes she'd thanked you properly and kept it instead of just eating it! She was really pleased that you picked it.'

George lowered his feathered front legs. 'She gave you that message for me?'

Jess nodded, too frightened to speak.

'Then I suppose you *must* know her,' he said grudgingly.

'How did you know all that, Jess?' Milly whispered.

'I, er, picked it up after Egypt,' she muttered vaguely, ignoring Michael's knowing look.

'We've been getting Fenella all sorts of things that will help her new egg,' Jason told George, 'which is why she gave us some gold. She wants silphium to place around the egg so her chick will be agile and strong . . .'

The gryphon frowned. 'Stuff and nonsense!

I'm telling you, that bird doesn't need silphium.
I mean, wherever did she get such an idea?'

'From a genie prophecy,' said Milly.

'Genies!' George tutted. 'Meddling misfits.'
He shook his head suddenly. 'Oh well. If
Fenella thinks she needs silphium then who am
I to argue or stand in her way? I'm just glad
she has another egg. I know it broke her heart
when she lost the first one.' He sighed. 'Very
well, children. As a gift to a dear friend . . . you
may take some back to her.'

'Oh, thank you!' Milly gasped.

Jason and Jess exchanged delighted looks.
Michael whistled in relief.

'Follow me,' said George.

He led them along the path to the banks
of a reedy river. Small rodents and insects
fled from the lush greenery as he approached.
There was a rocky outcropping with a waterfall
pouring down into the river of glittering water.
And there, at the edge of the riverbank, was
a large herb growing with flat yellow flowers
and feathery leaves.

George motioned to Milly. She walked
forward.

'We just need one stalk,' she said warily.

He carefully snapped off a leafy green strand
with his beak. 'There,' he said grandly, dropping
it into her hand.

'Thank you,' said Milly. 'We'll tell Fenella all about meeting you.'

The gryphon smiled at her broadly for a moment. 'You might suggest she comes to visit one day. With the new hatchling, perhaps.'

Milly was about to explain he would be waiting a long time – the Fenella they knew lived five hundred years in the future. But then who knew how long gryphons lived for? 'I'll tell her,' she promised.

She carried the herb back to the others, sweaty, dishevelled – and beaming all over her face.

'Thank you!' Jess called to the gryphon.

'Cheers, mate!' called Michael.

'Now you've got what you want, go away and stop bothering me,' said the gryphon. But Milly had a feeling that underneath his gruff-ness he was secretly glad to have seen them.

'Right, where's that feather, Jase?' said Michael, wiping the sweat from his forehead.

Jason held out the feather and they all grabbed hold. Milly took one last look around at the green forest with the birds in the trees, the butterflies flitting about, the waterfall cascading into the river beneath. She smiled at George, who was watching them, his eagle-like head held high, his tail swishing. Slowly, he smiled back at her, and a golden shimmer seemed to pass through his eyes.

'Bye!' she called.

'*Time before us, take us on.* Back to when we left!' Jason shouted, and the next moment he and the others were tumbling away through nothingness . . .

'Oh my poor little ducklings,' Fenella twittered as the children reappeared in the workshop. She was resting on the worktop. 'Look at you all, hot, wet and bothered! At least you're back in one piece though. You are in one piece, aren't you?'

Michael heaved himself off the floor. 'Think so.'

Jess nodded and rubbed her elbow where it had banged into the workbench on landing. 'We're OK.'

'We've got the herb, Fenella!' said Milly, waving it excitedly. 'And we saw George!'

'George!' Fenella's eyes lit up briefly. 'Oh my wings and tail feathers! I was hoping you'd meet him. I didn't like to say anything in case he wasn't there and you were disappointed. Did he take care of you then, dearies?'

'Take care!' exclaimed Michael, running his hands through his wet hair. 'More like gave us a heart attack!'

'He did save us from the cougar,' said

Milly, taking off her raincoat in the heat of the work shop. 'Even if he didn't quite mean to.'

'Oh, George always could be a bit cantankerous,' Fenella wheezed. 'But that was just his way. I missed him so much when he went to live in that rainforest.' She smiled sadly. 'I like to think he always had a soft spot for me though.'

'I think he did too,' said Milly, stroking her. 'When Jess told him about the sunset in wherever it was, and the cranberry gourd, he went a bit soppy.'

Fenella seemed pleased, but then she frown-ed. 'But how would you know about that, Jess lovey,' she said weakly, 'unless . . .'

Jess cringed. 'Um, you said about it, I think.'

'Did I, now?' Fenella gathered her breath and looked at her for a long moment. 'Well, if you say so, pet.'

'Are you OK?' Michael asked. 'You don't look well. You want to watch it.'

'Watch what?' Fenella looked baffled for a moment, but then she smiled. 'Aren't you lovely, Michael, worrying over an old bird like me. I'll be fine.' She coughed again. 'Truly, I will.'

The children swapped concerned looks. 'I hope so,' said Jess quietly.

'George must be a nice friend to have,' Milly said, hoping to lighten the mood. 'He's got a lovely smile, hasn't he?'

'He smiled at you?' Fenella clucked. 'It's said that the smile of a gryphon is a lucky charm. A very lucky charm indeed. You'll be coming in for some good fortune, my little chicklet, just you wait!'

Milly suddenly pictured herself crying in the car park after her audition, clutching onto Jess. *So much for good fortune,* she thought, but forced a smile of her own for Fenella. 'He was very nice. Maybe when you've been reborn and you're feeling strong again, you could go to the jungle and see him.'

'See him?' Fenella slowly shook her head and sighed. 'Oh, no. Time travels by, lovey. George'll be long gone by now. Him and his precious silphium.'

'Gone?' echoed Milly.

Fenella nodded. 'It isn't all fun being a fabulous bird who lives for ever, you know Friends come and go . . . Which is why I would so love to have a little hatchling to keep me company in the great long journey of never-ending life.' She glanced behind her at the kiln. 'Anyway!' She sounded as if she was trying to force some cheer into her voice. 'My nest's coming along nicely. Gold thread lining it. The egg resting on ash. Now silphium to shine the shell with. The only thing remaining is to get a drop of dew to moisten that little chick-abiddy's tongue the moment she pops her beak through.'

'We'll get it, Fenella,' Michael promised.

Jason nodded. 'We'll go tomorrow after school.'

Jess looked down at her soaking clothes. 'But right now, I think we need to go home and get changed.'

Milly nodded ruefully. 'My anorak is torn to bits. If Ann finds it she'll kill me. I think I'll leave it here.' She stuffed the anorak under a bench and looked about. 'Where shall I put the herb, Fenella?'

'Plonk it in my nest, lovey,' breathed Fenella. 'Ah, me, no wonder it was so sought after. Quickens the eye, speeds the body . . .' She stared dimly into the distance as if smiling at some sudden memory. 'It was banned from the third Olympic Games, you know.' Her voice was faint and slightly vacant. 'The discus hurler knocked out seven people with one throw. What a to-do there was . . .'

Ooooh, yes, that third Olympics . . . Jess groaned as the voice started in her head again. 'See you tomorrow, Fenella.'

'Though I expect you'll be *hearing* from me sooner,' said Fenella. 'Won't you, pet?'

Jess felt herself blushing. *She knows I took the ash*, she thought.

The phoenix waved a wing. 'Bye-bye, my love. And farewell, my fine young Michael.'

Michael smiled. 'Bye, Fenella.' He followed Jess outside, scratching his mosquito bites. 'Blimey, I need a bath. I just hope I'm not infectious . . .'

Milly and Jason lingered. Milly nudged Jason.

'Fenella?' he said slowly. 'Does silphium really help people to be better at sports and things?'

Fenella nodded. 'Oh yes, my little duckling, for a time. That was one of its boons, many years back.'

'It's just Jason's got a big football challenge tomorrow and he's not very good at football and he . . . we . . .' Milly took a deep breath. 'We were wondering if he could have just a tiny bit of the silphium—'

'No, Jason!' Jess exclaimed, bursting back through the doorway.

'Why not?' Jason retorted. 'I bet it would really help.'

'Magic always goes wrong!' exclaimed Jess.

'Oh, Jess, lovey,' clucked Fenella. 'You're such a worry-bucket. Life's too short.' She turned her head slowly and looked straight at

Jess with her dim eyes. 'Have you never taken chances, pet?'

'Maybe,' said Jess gloomily. 'But then I wished I hadn't.'

'Sometimes the only way to learn is from our mistakes,' said Fenella quietly. Then she coughed, shivered – and forced a smile for Jason. 'If you're worried and you really think you need help, then go on and have a nibble. Half a leaf should perk up your inner athlete.'

'Thanks, Fenella!' Jason said in delight. He quickly tore off a little of the leaf and thrust it in his mouth.

Jess turned away as Jason grimaced and swallowed it down . . .

Chapter Eighteen

Jason couldn't sleep that night. He'd gone to bed early, hoping the herb would magically go to work while he slept. Although he'd cleaned his teeth, he could still taste the leaf's bitterness on his tongue. *Perhaps that means my body is still absorbing it*, he thought, with a flutter of nerves. Tomorrow, he might just be able to kick a ball and run and dive like the other boys. He wouldn't be known just as 'geeky Jason' or the other mean names he'd been called most of his life.

He guessed the effect of the leaf would wear off eventually, but by then he'd hopefully have shown people what he could do and he wouldn't need to keep playing. They would ask him, plead with him to be on his team . . . *Nah, I wouldn't want to show up the rest of you*, he'd say modestly . . .

With a hopeful smile, he fell asleep.

But the next morning, Jason didn't feel any different. He sat next to Milly at the kitchen table and toyed with his half-eaten bowl of cereal.

'I'm really worried about Fenella,' Milly said. 'She looked awful last night when we got back from the jungle.'

'I know. She's getting weaker every day,' said Jason.

'She said it's normal but it's so horrid to watch,' sighed Milly. 'Oh, Jase. You do think her rebirth is going to be OK, don't you?'

He looked at her worriedly, for a moment forgetting about his own troubles. 'I hope so.'

Just then, the door opened and they quickly shut up but it was only Michael. He helped himself to a breakfast bar from the cupboard. 'Feeling sporty then?' he asked, looking at Jason.

'Not really,' Jason admitted.

'Oh, well. There are worse things than being a loser, mate.' Michael sniggered. 'I just can't think what they are right now.'

'You should know, Michael,' said Jess, breezing into the kitchen. 'Your mates are still teasing you over that whole mugging business.'

'They'll get over it!' Michael's voice turned pleading. 'I mean, they've got to. Haven't they?'

He shot a calculating look at Jason. 'Although maybe if *I* duff *you* up in public, the sniggering will stop.'

'Maybe we should be careful about drawing attention to ourselves in public,' said Jess quickly. 'Remember that spooky guy who was following us yesterday . . .'

'He hasn't really got in our way so far, has he?' said Michael. 'And tonight, we're gonna get the dewdrop – which means Fenella's shopping list is complete and whatever that bloke is watching us for, it won't matter.'

Milly got up and took her cereal bowl over to the sink. 'Just imagine – by tonight Fenella could be hatching her egg!'

Ann burst into the kitchen, car keys in her hand, a box of paperbacks under her arm. 'What's everyone hanging about for?' she cried. 'Go! School! NOW!'

For Jason the day crawled by. He was too nervous about the football challenge to eat much lunch. As the bell rang for the end of afternoon registration and he followed his class to the changing rooms, he felt a cloud of gloom gathering over him. He just wasn't any different. The herb hadn't worked. He was going to be as rubbish as always in the football tournament.

The girl in front, Susan Walsh, was carrying her bag at an angle, and Jason noticed her denim pencil case falling out. Suddenly time seemed to slow down around him. As the case slipped free, Jason darted out one foot almost without thinking – and neatly caught the case on the toe of his shoe!

'What a fluke!' someone said beside him.

Susan turned and gave him a puzzled smile as he passed it to her. 'Thanks, Jason.'

He blushed.

'Pity you can't do that with a ball, Worthington,' grunted Bradley Mantle, tall, curly-haired captain of the under-ten football team, as he pushed past. He had never talked to Jason before in his life.

Jason felt a prickle of delight. *Maybe, Bradley,* he thought, *you're in for a surprise.*

Ten minutes later, the Years Four, Five and Six mixed football tournament was getting underway. The younger kids were being excused from lessons so they could watch and make some noise for the different teams, and Milly was keeping a watchful eye on Jason. He was standing about, looking oddly excited, and when he saw her, he gave her a big thumbs-up. Milly waved madly.

The teachers divided the pupils into teams of seven, ready to play each other in rotation.

Milly saw that Jason was on a team with Bradley Mantle, and her heart sank. Jason wouldn't get a look in with the sportiest kid in the school hogging the limelight.

Jason jogged on the spot. Now he was moving around on the playing field, he felt strong and fit. 'Who's playing where, Bradley?'

'I'll play up front,' said Bradley. 'Paul, Sean, you play across the middle. Tony, get in goal. Gilbo, Kemp, you're at the back. Worthington . . . just stay out of the way, OK?'

The whistle blew. 'Go, Jase!' Milly yelled.

Jason was off like a rocket towards the goal.

'I said, stay out of the way!' Bradley yelled.

But Jason didn't want to stop. He'd never felt so full of energy before. 'To me!' he shouted to Sean, who had taken possession of the ball.

Sean hesitated but then crossed it to Jason.

Jason stuck his foot out and just managed to get his toe to the ball. *Now, it's a team game,* he told himself. *I suppose I'd better pass it too.* He saw Paul outrunning two defenders and booted the ball towards him. But his aim was off, the pass went wide – and to his amazement, the ball flew towards the goal, missed the keeper's hands by centimetres and thumped into the back of the net.

Milly almost exploded with delight. 'YES!'

Jason stared in shock as a big cheer went up.

He had scored a goal! He'd actually scored a goal!

'Nice one, Jason!' Sean shouted.

'Fluke,' Bradley spat.

Maybe it was, thought Jason, glowing as the onlookers went on clapping. *But next time I'll mean to score one!*

The goalie kicked the ball forward but Bradley managed to get his head to it, brought it down and set off down the left wing.

'To me!' Jason shouted, jumping up and down on the penalty spot, waving his arms.

Bradley crossed the ball.

But Mr Hurst, the referee, blew his whistle. 'Offside! No goal hanging, Jason. You'd gone past the last defender when Bradley crossed the ball – that's offside.'

'Nice work, Worthington,' said Bradley sourly, shaking his head. 'That's a free kick to them, you muppet.'

Jason ran back to his own half. OK, so he might not know all the rules – but he'd already scored one goal, and he was going to score another!

Susan Walsh took the free kick. She tried to play it to someone on her team, but Jason raced over and slid in, neatly stopping the ball with his shins. He jumped to his feet and swivelled on the spot, eyeing up the ball. He was going to show everyone what he could do! He thwacked the ball as hard as he could.

It soared through the air like a black-and-white meteor and crashed against the crossbar so hard it knocked the whole goal over. The ball ricocheted off and struck Mr Hurst in the stomach – he fell over backwards and almost swallowed his whistle.

Bradley stared at Jason. 'What was *that* meant to be?'

'Um, the wind must have got behind it,' said Jason weakly. 'Sorry, Mr Hurst!'

Mr Hurst was too short of breath to answer. Another teacher was helping him to his feet. The goalie and two defenders struggled to right the goal.

Milly bit her lip. Jason had the power, but it seemed he hadn't worked out quite how to use it. 'Go, Jase!' she called again, only a little more quietly this time.

Jason wiped his sweating hands on his top while he and his fellow players waited for Mr Hurst to recover. Several dirty looks were shot his way as the delay dragged on, and Jess's words rang in his ears – *Magic always goes wrong when we try to use it for ourselves.*

'Not this time,' he muttered determinedly.

Mr Hurst, with a wary look at Jason, had recovered enough to blow his whistle again.

Play resumed as the other team's goalie booted the ball down the pitch. Jason duly hared after it, outrunning both opposing midfielders.

'Unmarked!' yelled Bradley from the far touchline.

But Jason wasn't about to give up the ball to Bradley now he'd got it. Susan Walsh was making straight for him. If he could just chip the ball over her head, dodge past and try to head it in himself . . .

He got his toe neatly under the ball and flicked it up hard. It smacked into Susan's chin and bounced off, heading straight for Jason's face. He ducked automatically, and the ball struck a boy behind him instead. With a cry, the boy went down. Susan was already lying on the ground, groaning and clutching her chin. Jason stared round in confusion – and one of the opposition nicked in and tried to take the ball. Jason swung a leg wildly but missed the ball completely, upending the player instead.

'Foul!' someone yelled.

'I didn't mean to!' Jason protested.

Mr Hurst blew his whistle. 'All right, Jason. Take a time out – for all our sakes!'

Milly looked on, dismayed, as Jason walked away from the carnage he had caused to the edge of the pitch, his cheeks burning. As the fallen players staggered back up, play resumed and

Bradley soon scored a goal. The crowd erupted in cheers again.

Standing alone as a fine rain began to fall, Jason listened to the applause and his heart sank slowly down into his football boots. Forget being rubbish at sport – now everyone must think he was a total freak. He'd wanted to make things better but he'd made them much worse.

'Jason Worthington, magical football hero,' he muttered unhappily to himself. 'NOT.'

Chapter Nineteen

'I don't want to talk about it,' Jason announced, hurrying on ahead of Michael, Jess and Milly as they all made their way to Mr Milton's house after school.

'Milly said that you sucked,' called Michael.

'I didn't!' Milly protested. 'I just said you were . . . um . . . unlucky.'

'*And* that you sucked,' Michael persisted.

'You should have seen his goal, Michael,' said Milly, glaring at her brother. 'It was amazing!'

'I was trying to pass to Paul,' muttered Jason through gritted teeth. He stopped and let the girls catch up. 'I suppose those athletes at the third Olympic Games Fenella mentioned did so well with the herb because they were trained athletes to start off with and could use the extra power it gave them – they weren't rubbish like me. You were right, Jess, I shouldn't have taken it – aren't you going to say you told me so?'

Jess looked tired and bad-tempered. 'No. But I *could* say the name of every athlete who took part in the third Olympics, what events they won and how many of them had a bald spot right on top of their heads.' Her voice slowly began to rise. 'Just as I can tell you the phoenix name for a hundred and fifty different shapes of cloud, which part of the sky tastes the sweetest and how Fenella spotted the young Abraham Lincoln canoeing down the Sangamon River and dropped an apple into his boat to keep his strength up!'

Milly and Jason stared at her in alarm.

'She ate some of that phoenix ash,' explained Michael. 'To get phoenix wisdom.'

'And now every time I think of *anything* I hear Fenella's memory of it in my head. It's driving me crazy!' Jess held up her hands. 'I know, I know – I was stupid to do it but like Jason with that herb, like Michael and his gold, I was looking for a magic fix to solve all my exam worries – a short cut to take me to a better place.' She snorted. 'I should have known better!'

'How come you told Michael and not us?' Milly asked, hurt.

'I told Michael on the way to school. I was

going to tell you later but then when it didn't work out, I just felt . . . stupid. Completely stupid. I'm sorry.' Jess took a deep breath and set off again. 'Now, come on, Fenella will be waiting for us.'

'Does she know you tasted the ash?' Jason asked, hurrying after her.

'I think so,' admitted Jess. 'She kind of hinted at it yesterday. I've decided I'm going to say sorry when we see her.' She rubbed her forehead. 'And then I'm going to ask if she knows how I can get rid of it!'

'At least we haven't seen that bloke again,' said Jason.

'He's probably been watching us like Skribble said, seen what a bunch of doofuses we all are, and gone off laughing,' Michael remarked.

They crossed the road and walked down Mr Milton's drive. Mr Milton himself was there beside a copse of trees, fussing over one of his statues. When he saw the children he started towards them.

'Here we go,' Michael muttered. 'Be-kind-to-loony-OAPs day is here again.'

'Michael, don't be horrible,' hissed Jess, but at the same time she had to suppress a grin.

'Goodness, children, back visiting already!' Mr Milton glanced round at them. 'I'm terribly impressed with your dedication. I would be very interested to see the fruits of all these hours you're spending in my workshop.'

'Oh, we're not very good,' said Milly hastily. 'We've had to, er, throw away most of what we've done.'

'Then perhaps I can give you some hints and tips,' Mr Milton suggested in a kindly way. 'Although, I'm afraid to say, the kiln is going to be taken out of action tomorrow. The men are coming to fix it.' He smiled hopefully. 'However, that needn't mean you have to stay away from the house. I would be very happy to entertain you. Please do drop in any time you wish.'

'Um, yes, that sounds great,' said Jess awkwardly. 'We'll tell Mum and maybe she can organize something.'

'Thank you again for letting us use your workshop,' Milly said. 'Thanks for everything.'

'You are more than welcome, my dear.' Mr Milton smiled. 'Believe a lonely old man when he says – the pleasure and the benefit is mine.'

He hobbled away and they walked on to the workshop. 'We'd better get the dewdrop this afternoon,' said Milly, feeling worried as she pushed open the door. 'If the kiln is being turned off tomorrow then Fenella won't have anywhere and . . .' She trailed off and her hands flew to her mouth. '*Fenella?*'

A feathered figure lay shivering on the workbench. But it was barely recognizable as the Fenella they knew. Her golden feathers had tarnished and discoloured to a mottled grey. Several had fallen out in a spiky pile beside her. Her beak was resting on the bench, her eyes were shut and she seemed to be barely breathing.

'What's happened?' gasped Milly.

'The kiln door's closed,' Jess realized. 'She must have been shut out.' Grabbing a towel from the bench, she tried the handle and the door readily opened. She flinched as a wave of heat burst out from inside.

'The egg's all right,' said Jason, peering inside.

'And so's her nest,' Jess noted, lifting some bits of newspaper from the gold-laced den of twigs tucked away behind the kiln.

'Poor Fenella,' Milly murmured.

Michael stroked the bird's head. It felt icy cold.

'Michael?' The phoenix's eyes fluttered open, a pale and watery blue. 'Is that you, lovey?'

'Yes. Everything's OK.' Michael nodded encouragingly. 'We're here now.'

'I went out for a few more sticks for the nest,' Fenella whispered. 'The door of the kiln swung shut. I couldn't open it again, try as I might . . .' She gave a throaty cough. 'Oh, just look at me.' Her eyes closed again. 'Weaker than a one-legged sparrow. I've never felt like this before . . .'

'Let's get you back into the kiln where it's warm,' said Jess, placing her own hand on the phoenix's cold feathers.

'Wait!' Fenella's eyes fixed on Jess. 'You tasted the ash of my nest, didn't you?'

Jess nodded awkwardly. 'I was going to tell you. I . . .'

'Did it bring you happiness, pet?' Fenella asked. There was hopefulness, not accusation in the phoenix's cloudy eyes. 'I hope it did. You've been so kind to an old bird, made me so happy . . . I only ever wanted the four of you to be happy in return.' A tear left a gleaming trail over her cold feathers. 'Jason, I hope the herb helped you, love. And Milly, you must taste a little of the dewdrop if you find it. Help that dear singing voice of yours along a little.'

Milly wiped her nose, not trusting herself to speak. *It won't make any difference,* she thought, and right now it didn't seem to matter anyway.

'And Michael?' Fenella raised her head, looking about, confused. 'Are you there?'

'I'm here,' he said, a lump in his throat as he put his fingers against one of her claws.

At his touch, Fenella smiled. 'What is it you'd

like? Should I spin you more gold? I would, you know, if you'd be happy . . .'

Michael felt tears burn his eyes and heard Milly sniff beside him. 'Fenella . . .' he muttered.

'I know,' she whispered. 'Happiness can be a hard thing to pin down.'

Jess smiled ruefully. 'As hard as pinning down tomorrow's sunshine.'

'As I fade, pet, so will my voice in your head. I'll be back with a new voice soon, just you wait . . . and hopefully with a fine, upstanding hatchling beside me, thanks to you and your brothers and sister.' She coughed again. 'Thank you . . . for helping me.'

Jason cleared his throat. 'Just hang in there, Fenella. We'll get you what you need.'

He put on the thick, insulated gloves from the workbench. Michael carefully lifted Fenella and placed her in Jason's hands. Jason put her inside the kiln beside her egg, and Jess gently closed the door.

'We'd better get after this dewdrop,' Milly said. 'And fast!'

Michael sighed. 'We don't even know which feather to use.'

'This one.' Jess selected a long, mottled feather from the spiky heap. 'It's from her right wing. It'll get us there.'

'And where exactly *is* there, anyway?' Michael asked. 'I've never heard of Mount Quamquangle.'

'It's a phoenix name,' Jess explained. 'Really it's a remote glacier in Patagonia, near to Argentina, also known as the Whispering Peak. They're about four hours behind us, and we need to get there at dawn, so we'll have to travel about seven hours into the past.'

Michael gave her a small smile. 'Wow. So phoenix wisdom comes in handy for something.'

Jess nodded, reached into her bag and pulled out fleeces for everyone. 'It's going to be very wet and cold up there, so I brought us these.'

They all slipped on the extra layers of clothing.

'I'm going to wear my torn anorak too for extra protection,' said Milly, pulling out the crumpled cream jacket from under the bench and slipping it on over the fleece.

'I brought two pipettes to collect the dewdrop,' Jason announced.

'Pipettes?' Milly echoed.

'From my chemistry set,' he explained, producing a tiny glass tube with a soft yellow rubber teat on one end. 'A pipette draws up liquid and stores it till you can transfer it to somewhere else.'

'Why two of them?' asked Michael.

'Because I'm useless, remember?' Jason smiled ruefully. 'I broke my magnifying glass before – and there won't be a future me to help out on top of Mount Quamquangle if I break the pipette!'

Michael nodded. 'Good thinking.'

'So, let's go!' Jess held up the feather, and Michael, Milly and Jason took hold of it too. '*Time of yore, be never gone* – take us to seven hours ago, on the summit of Mount Quamquangle!'

The now familiar sparkles of gold light shot through Jess's vision as she felt herself begin to drift away, falling through space . . .

Then, with a crunch of hard-packed snow, she arrived with the others – balanced precariously on a misty mountaintop. It was freezing cold and the sky was the colour of wet charcoal, just beginning to lighten with the first rays of dawn. The wind howled in lonely, heartbreaking notes, almost like music. Rainclouds gusted past like ghosts, spurning the barren mountainside for kinder climes. Already Milly felt short of breath. She wished she was back in the warm, dry workshop.

'We can't see a thing,' Michael shouted over the gale. 'And there's snow and ice everywhere. How are we going to find a dewdrop?'

Jason had the map out already, and tapped at a red X pulsating in the top right corner. 'This way,' he said, pointing ahead of them.

'Be careful not to slip,' Jess warned.

'I'm not sure dew can even form at this kind of altitude,' said Jason, shivering as he moved surely over the frozen surface.

'You can bet your bum it's magic dew,' said Michael.

'Be careful, you two,' Jess called after him. 'What we're looking for is up ahead.'

A large shadowy shape loomed up. Michael yelled: 'It's a yeti!'

Milly shrieked.

'Actually it's not,' Jason added quickly. 'It's . . . a statue.'

'Maybe we should tell Mr Milton,' said Michael, acting cool again after his little outburst. 'He could do it up for us.'

Hugging herself for warmth, Milly slipped and slid closer. She couldn't help but gasp as the rainclouds seemed to roll away and reveal a strange but beautiful sculpture carved from black, windblown rock. It was a stone cascade of loops and spirals, like some spidery octopus with endless tentacles, standing bigger than a man. Drops of moisture stood proud on the dark surface like beads of sweat.

'I don't like this,' Milly whispered. 'Who built it?'

'An ancient tribe of summit dwellers,' Jess reported. 'Fenella met with them once, so long ago . . . A few hundred years back she came looking for them again. But the people had all gone and only this statue was left.' She shrugged. 'Anyway, this is where the dew formed. We need to find the very first drop.'

'Half of it's rain!' Michael protested, stamping his feet as he peered at the statue. 'It's like picking out a special piece of hay from a haystack.'

The wind blew stronger, but as it whipped through the loops and whorls in the huge stone statue, its accusing howl grew softer – to Milly's ears, almost a whisper. The same word, whispered over and over in a voice like the sea dragging slates across a shore.

'*Beware* . . .'

'What was that?' Milly demanded, staring all around. She could see Jess, Michael, Jason and the statue clearly enough, but the shrouding mists hid all else from view. 'It sounded like a voice . . .'

'They called it the whispering summit, way back when,' Jess reminded her. 'It's just the wind.'

But again, the harsh whisper struck up in the stone. '*Beware eyes behind glass* . . .'

'I think I heard something too,' said Michael.

'It *is* a voice,' Milly insisted, but Jess shushed her as the whispering started up again.

'*Do not take the dewdrop . . .*'

'Something wants us to leave,' said Jason uneasily.

'But we have to get the dewdrop first!' protested Milly. 'We can't let Fenella down.'

'Quickly,' said Jess, walking around the statue. She could hear the phoenix wisdom in her mind: *Those dear old mountain peoples! I had such a chinwag with their chief back in my earliest days. He would climb to the summit each day and taste the first dewdrop that formed on the magical shape of stone. Fancy! 'Every day we see the world anew,' he told me. 'And if we are ever to learn, then every day we must forget what we know and learn it afresh.' He was a dear man. He told me once, 'I can always tell the true drop by the glimmer of gold within . . .'*

Jess shook her head to clear it of Fenella's voice. 'The first dewdrop has a glimmer of gold.'

Jason peered closely at the stone, but a vengeful gust of wind blew cold, stinging rain into his face.

The spooky voice hissed out with the rain: '*Leave here now, and learn another's truth . . .*'

'This stone thing is definitely talking.' Michael backed away. 'That is so not good.'

'We're not taking the dew for ourselves,' Jess shouted over the rising howl of the wind.

A savage gust knocked Milly off balance, and she fell to her knees before the statue. She stared in surprise at a scintilla of sunlight caught in one of the raindrops. It reminded her of Fenella's glow jewel.

'Jess,' Milly shouted. 'I think I've found the golden one!'

Jess crouched down to see and nodded excitedly. 'You have! Oh, well done, Milly!'

The voice swelled to a blustering shout. '*BEWARE* . . .'

'Our friend can't hatch her egg without it!' Milly yelled up at the statue.

Then she noticed Jason had pulled out his pipette with the yellow teat. 'Here we go then!' he cried.

'But that drop is tiny, and there are so many others around it!' Jess called. 'And you have to get the whole of the drop, Jason.'

'No pressure then, mate,' Michael called.

Jason slowly raised the pipette. 'The silphium may not have done wonders for my inner athlete, but that's because I've had no athlete's training . . .'

'But you've been training to be a geek your

whole life!' Michael realized. 'Cool! Go for it!'

The voices blew and billowed up around them and the wind itself seemed to carry a new note of warning.

'*Beware eyes behind glass . . .*'

'*Do not take the dew . . .*'

'*Beware false lines on parchment . . .*'

'Don't let the voices put you off, Jason,' Jess urged him.

Faster than a striking cobra, Jason stabbed down at the stone with the pipette and then drew back his hand. 'Got it!'

Abruptly, the wind dropped and died away to nothing. The clouds shrank away from the statue, as if suddenly afraid. Sunlight, golden and cruel, flooded down over the barren, silent summit of Mount Quamquangle. The children looked at each other uneasily.

'Sunlight,' said Michael quietly. 'Well, that's meant to be a good omen, isn't it?'

No one replied. The sudden calm felt unnatural, like feeling the crisp freshness after a storm when there had *been* no storm. *Like we took a short cut*, Jess thought privately. *Again.*

Jason put the pipette carefully into a test tube and placed it in his pocket.

'I think I'd like to go back now,' said Milly quietly.

Jess pulled out the feather, and they each took hold.

'*Time before us, take us on*,' Michael commanded. 'To our starting point, seven hours from now.'

Milly smiled gratefully as the golden speckles of the magical feather crept into her view, brighter than the thin mountain sunlight. She was glad when the barren crag faded from her sight, but as the workshop came back into existence around them, the shadow of the statue seemed to linger in her vision. The statue that gazed down over all, from the top of the world . . .

'Warmth!' gasped Michael, stamping up and down, trying to get the circulation going in his legs. 'Wow, was that ever cold.'

Jason let go of the feather and checked his watch. 'It only took us thirty minutes.'

Milly beamed through chattering teeth. 'George the gryphon's smile must really have brought us good luck!'

'We've got the lot,' Jess declared. 'Tomorrow's sunlight, the ash of Fenella's old nest, the silphium and the dewdrop.'

'The full package,' Michael agreed.

'Fenella will be so pleased,' said Jason as Jess slipped on the oven gloves and started to open the door.

'We've got everything you asked for, Fenella!' Milly cried. 'You and your egg are going to be—'

Her voice choked off as the door swung open and she saw that the kiln was empty.

Michael frowned. 'I don't believe it.'

'She's gone,' Milly whispered, staring in shock. 'Fenella, the nest and her egg – they've disappeared!'

Chapter Twenty

'Fenella can't have just gone!' said Jess, looking around. 'She must be here somewhere.'

'Wait,' said Jason. 'Look, the kiln's not working. The power's cut off.'

'This is weird,' said Michael uneasily. 'No bird. No egg. No nest. No power.'

'Let's look at the map,' Milly suggested. She wrapped her ragged anorak more closely around her, still feeling some of the mountain chill in her bones. 'If something's lost, the map always shows us where it is.'

Jason pulled the map out of his pocket and unfolded it. It had changed once again. Now there was a small building marked in one corner and the rest of the paper was taken up with a much larger building crisscrossed with lines. It looked like lots of rooms overlaid on top of each other with corridors in-between.

'It's a house,' Jason said. 'I think it's Mr Milton's house – and the small building is the workshop.'

'And that must be Fenella!' said Michael, stabbing his finger down on a red cross in the middle of the big building.

'So what's this?' said Milly, pointing to another much smaller cross marked on the map.

'I bet it's the egg in the nest,' said Michael.

'But why are they in Mr Milton's house?' asked Jason.

They were all silent for a moment, each of them frowning, lost in worried thoughts.

Milly's face was pale. 'Do you . . . do you think something bad might have happened?'

Michael shrugged helplessly. 'She wasn't looking too hot last time we saw her.'

'Hot,' Jess echoed. 'Of course, if the kiln has packed up, she might have gone looking for warmth in Mr Milton's house.'

'She might be in his oven,' said Jason anxiously. 'We've got to find her!'

Milly was already racing across the lawn. Jason pulled away from Michael and Jess and caught up with her easily, barely out of breath. In a single athletic bound, he leaped up the five stone steps that led to the back of the house and ran up to the big French windows that led inside. They stood ajar, but he hesitated. 'I suppose we can't just go in, can we?'

Jess lingered at the foot of the steps. 'Maybe we should go round the front and knock.'

'And say what?' asked Michael. 'Sorry, Mr Milton, but there's an invisible phoenix flying around your house, can we have her back, please? Oh, and we need to look for her egg on the way!'

Milly shrugged. 'He said we could drop in any time, didn't he?'

'But then he'll take us to his living room so he and his old duffer mate can bore us to death,' Michael pointed out. 'I say we go straight in and find Fenella.'

Jason looked at the map. The big red cross was right in the centre. 'Michael's right. Fenella might need that dewdrop right now.'

'If we run into Mr Milton, we could say we came to say bye or something,' Milly said with sudden inspiration. 'Anyway, if the door's open it might mean he's in the garden. He usually is.'

They glanced about but there was no sign of the old man.

'Someone should stay out here as lookout, just in case he is outside,' said Jess.

'You stay, Mil,' said Michael. She opened her mouth to argue but he shushed her. 'You can wind people round your little finger, you know you can. If old Milton comes along

232

you'll be able to make up some sort of story and distract him while we get out.'

Milly's frown softened. 'I suppose so.'

'That's a really good idea.' Jess nodded. 'Maybe you should stay out here too, Jason.'

Jason shook his head. 'We might need to climb up and get Fenella or something. Then my extra agility might come in useful.'

'OK, the three of us will go.' Jess reached into her pocket. 'Here, take my mobile, Milly. Ring Michael if you see Mr Milton.'

Milly took it quickly. 'I will.'

'Meanwhile we'll go in and get Fenella – and the egg,' said Michael. He looked at the others. 'Let's go!'

Leaving Milly on the look out, Michael, Jess and Jason moved cautiously into a large sitting room. The smell of furniture polish hung in the warm, still air. The walls were panelled in old dark wood. It felt very strange to be standing there – *strange and wrong*, Jess thought, her skin prickling.

There were big double doors on the other side of the room. Michael nodded at them and Jess and Jason followed him over. Michael turned the handle and they found themselves looking into a long corridor lined with portraits in ornate gold frames.

Jason got the map out. 'I think we're here,'

he whispered, pointing to the map. He traced a winding route from where they were to the biggest red cross with his finger. 'And this is where we have to go.'

'Lead the way then, mate,' Michael said in a low voice. 'You're the whiz with maps.'

With Jason in the lead, they set off down the corridor. Jess half expected Mr Milton to open a door at any moment and see them. Her breath felt short in her throat, her palms were sweating. What would they say to him? 'One, two, three . . .' Jason muttered, counting the doorways as they went. *'Four!* I think we have to go through this room!'

Michael put his hand on the door and slowly opened it. It led into a small sitting room. The curtains were closed and the furniture was covered in sheets. On the other side there was another door. When they went through it they found themselves in another corridor.

'This place is like a maze,' Jess whispered.

They turned right and went down the corridor before going up three steps. They passed strange objects on the landing – a tiger skin was hung on one wall, its mouth wide. There was an old dusty roundabout horse in one corner. A stuffed crocodile in a glass case lay in another, glaring beadily at them. A display of old medical instruments cluttered a tabletop.

Several times the corridor split into two and they had to choose whether to go left or right. Jess's head began to spin. She didn't like the twisty, turning corridor, didn't like all this weird old bric-a-brac. 'Are you still following where we are on the map?' she asked Jason in a low voice.

He nodded. 'Fenella should be in the next room on the right.'

They reached the room and paused. Michael listened. 'There's no sound,' he reported, and slowly opened the door.

They were in a study with a big desk and bookshelves. The chair had been pushed back and a pen was lying by some paper without its top on. There was a half-drunk glass of water. It looked as if someone had been there recently.

'Fenella!' called Jess softly.

The three of them looked around. 'She's not here,' said Michael.

'I'm sure this was where the map wanted us to go,' said Jason. He looked down at the parchment and cried out.

'What is it?' Jess asked in alarm.

Wordlessly, Jason held out the map, and Jess and Michael both gasped.

The parchment was blank. Every line, every marking, had completely vanished.

A cold feeling shivered over Michael's skin. 'How could that happen?' He took the parchment to check the other side – but at his touch it crumbled like stale flaky pastry.

'The map!' Jess cried. 'You clumsy—'

'It wasn't my fault,' Michael protested, staring at the brittle fragments that were all that was left of the map. 'It just fell apart.'

Jason picked up a piece and it disintegrated. 'Maybe – maybe it ran out of magic.'

Jess felt sick. 'What if this means we're too late? What if Fenella . . . ?'

'Don't,' said Michael through gritted teeth. 'She's OK. She's got to be—'

Suddenly a squeal of hinges tore through the air. The door to the room was swinging shut.

In a flash, on instinct, Jason dashed across the room and stood in the doorway. But the door was still trying to close, as though someone invisible was leaning against it.

'Quick, get out!' Jason gasped. 'I can't hold it.'

Michael and Jess bundled out through the closing gap. Jason moved aside with them – and the door banged shut.

'What was *that* all about?' Michael whispered.

'I don't know,' said Jess. 'This all feels really wrong.'

Jason nodded. 'Let's go back the way we came.'

They set off down the gloomy passage. But it was hard to remember which way to turn and which rooms to go through.

'I don't remember that,' Jess said, pointing to a glass case of stuffed snakes.

'Me neither,' said Michael anxiously.

The more they wandered around, the more bewildered they felt. Jess felt panic clawing inside her. 'What happened to the stairs?'

'It's like they've vanished,' Michael said grimly.

'The house *can't* be this big,' Jason said miserably; 'it just can't be!'

'We're lost,' Jess agreed. 'Completely and utterly lost!'

Milly had spent the first five minutes after the others had gone looking eagerly around for any sign of Mr Milton. But when he failed to appear, she sat down on the stone steps, feeling bored.

It was dull being here on her own, and she couldn't wait to see Fenella again and show her the dewdrop.

She's going to be so happy, Milly thought. *We've got everything she needs now to hatch her chick.*

Of course, Fenella had urged her to taste the dewdrop. Could it really help her to sing? She knew that she wouldn't be Annie – but was that because she did taste the dewdrop, or because she didn't? How could she ever know?

She sighed, tired from trying to make sense of it all. Where were the others? She took the mobile out of her pocket and called Michael. The call went straight through to Michael's voicemail.

Maybe there's no signal inside the house, Milly thought. She went to the door. Perhaps she should go after them . . .

But as she reached the door she heard a sound that made her freeze. It was halfway between a squawk and a loud shriek.

Fenella! Milly thought.

The sound rent the air again. It seemed to be coming from outside somewhere, round the corner of the house. *She must have got back out*, Milly thought as she leaped down the steps, her heart pounding. And it sounded as if the phoenix was in trouble.

Milly didn't stop to think. She charged across the paving stones and round the side of the house. She hadn't seen this part before. There was a pale octagonal stone building linked to the house by a covered passage. The building had leaded windows on each of its eight sides. One of them was open and through it came another horrible cry.

Milly raced up to the building. She was about to burst through the door when common sense suddenly gripped her. What if someone – or

238

something – was threatening Fenella? Something really bad?

She ran to the window instead and peered in.

Fenella, her feathers still pale and tarnished, was perched on a stone table right in the centre – and Mr Milton was in there too! He had his back to her and was picking something up from one of eight cluttered workbenches lining the room. What was going on? Maybe Fenella had flown inside and then Mr Milton had found her there . . .

Milly frowned as she suddenly noticed a locked manacle around Fenella's leg. It was attached by a chain to a stout metal ring in the centre of the table. The phoenix seemed to gather her strength and rose up into the air, wings flapping, shrieking loudly as she fought against the chain.

Goose pimples prickled across Milly's skin. What was going on?

'Be quiet, phoenix!' snapped Mr Milton, swinging round. His eyes met Milly's through the window. 'Ah, hello, my dear,' he said, with that familiar smile. 'I'm so glad you decided to call by.'

He reached out one hand in her direction and clenched his fist. Milly felt her throat tighten. She gasped as her vision spun and her legs buckled beneath her . . .

And suddenly she was *inside* the octagonal room, sprawled on the patterned stone floor, looking up at Mr Milton. And in a heartbeat, the old man had changed. Gone were the old tweedy clothes – now he was wearing an expensive dark suit and a black fez with two white tassels. He was no longer stooped, but seemed tall and powerful.

'The board is set, the players are assembled . . .' The smile on Mr Milton's face twisted into a cruel leer. 'Let the final game begin.'

Chapter Twenty-One

'Get away, pet,' Fenella croaked from the table. 'Run, lovey, run!'

Milly jumped to her feet, but as she turned back to the open window it slammed shut with a loud bang. Mr Milton chuckled softly. It wasn't a pleasant sound.

'I don't understand,' Milly said, looking up at him, her mind still struggling to accept the change in him. 'You seemed so nice . . .'

Milton arched an eyebrow. 'Would you have come here with your phoenix had I been bad-tempered or aloof? I had to seem to be a harmless, lonely old man of whom you could take advantage.' He snorted. 'You thought you were tricking me wonderfully, didn't you? That I was unknowingly providing you with the perfect home for your golden friend.' His face hardened. 'But all the time, I was the one pulling the strings.'

Milly stared, realizing how completely they had been fooled. 'So you knew Fenella would come to us and you made friends with my stepmum and took us to your workshop, just so we would know about it and think of it as a hiding place?'

He nodded. 'And, gracious me, the kiln was jammed on full blast, twenty-four hours a day. How convenient!'

'I thought it was destiny,' croaked Fenella.

Mr Milton's eyes glinted. 'Ah, but your destiny is to serve me – all of you!'

Fenella launched herself into flight, straining once more against her chain. 'Quickly, lovey!' she squawked to Milly. 'I'll distract him, you run!'

'No! I won't leave you!' Milly cried.

'And you, phoenix, are going nowhere.' Milton reached out, grabbed Fenella by the neck and hauled her roughly back down to the table where she lay panting for breath. 'After all, you don't want to miss a happy reunion between a girl and a worm, do you?' He laughed, crossed to the nearest workbench and picked up an object that Milly recognized in a heart-stopping second. It was a brass lamp with a round body and a long tall spout. The handle was twisted and had a snake's head rearing up at the end of it.

'The genie lamp,' Milly breathed. '*Skribble's* lamp?'

'My aged guest – or, more accurately, my prisoner.' Milton plucked out the brass stopper.

'Ho, worm! Are you still in there, you cringing cur?'

Milly forgot her own predicament and Fenella's for a moment. 'Don't you talk to Skribble like that!' she shouted.

'I will talk to him as I choose,' said Milton calmly. 'For he is in my power. I took the lamp when you placed it in that junk shop, you see. I summoned the genie.' He held the spout to his lips and raised his voice. 'You have no choice, do you, Skribbaleum! Not now I have command-ed from you an endless stream of wishes that must be granted!' He rubbed the lamp disdainfully on the sleeve of his suit and, in a purple puff of smoke, Skribble appeared, just as he had done outside the workshop, a tiny moustached figure in a cloak and turban floating on an iridescent cloud. He looked worried and furious in equal measure.

'Milly,' Skribble cried. 'And Fenella, are you all right? Has this misanthropic microbe harmed you in any way?'

'Harm them, wormish one?' Milton laughed. 'Does a craftsman damage his tools before he begins work?'

'These are not tools,' Skribble stormed. 'They are living things, marvellous and magical. The girl is but a child—'

'And most necessary,' Milton interrupted. 'Which is why I've separated her from her siblings.'

Milly swallowed down her frightened tears as she looked at her beloved bookworm. 'Oh, Skribble, why didn't you warn us more that something was wrong when you came to us?'

'Milton *compelled* me to go to you,' said Skribble wretchedly. 'He is the wish-maker and by my genie oath I can do nothing but serve him. He wished that I would appear to you to keep you focused on your quest – but forbade me from warning you of his true nature.'

'I remember,' Milly groaned. 'You found it hard to speak . . . But you warned us somebody was watching. We just didn't think you meant Mr Milton!'

Skribble sighed. 'I could sense that Michael had doubts about him. I tried to make him look at the words I had placed on the map right from the start: know yourself, trust yourself, *believe* in yourself – and not in me. I couldn't be clearer because of the wish but, oh! How I wanted to say more!' The worm shook his head. 'Forgive me, my dear Milly . . . and please, Fenella, forgive me also. For I have been forced to deceive you all along, right from our first encounter in Morocco . . .'

Fenella blinked incredulously.

'The worm was my puppet,' Milton hissed. 'That prophecy of the egg he shared with you was entirely *my* invention. I wished of my genie that he fool you into thinking it had come from the Great Library . . . and naturally he had no choice but to obey.' He gave her a jackal's smile. 'For centuries now I have been planning . . . plotting . . . planting the seeds of my eventual triumph!'

Milly stared. 'Centuries? But how can you be that old?'

'Once,' put in Skribble, '"Mr Milton" – or to call him by his real name, Miltakbar Memesis the Thrice-Born – was a genie himself. Yes, by all accounts a very great genie indeed, way back when even I was but a stripling.'

'A great genie?' Milton snorted, threw back his head and set his fez tassels twitching. 'You wrong me, worm – I was master of all!'

Milly was struggling to take in so many revelations. 'He's a *genie*! But then how come he's got a hold on you, Skribble? I thought genies weren't able to work magic on each other!'

'He is a genie no longer,' Skribble explained. 'The magic he now possesses was stolen from the human world in the dark, savage times of old.' The worm scowled. 'Many centuries ago, he and his witch-bride attempted to overthrow the Genie Council. Their revolution was crushed, and this would-be master's magic was taken from him. He was sentenced to walk the earth in

245

mortal form for ever. As for his charmless lady-friend—'

'Cringing worm!' Milton stormed. 'If you must speak of my queen you'll do so with respect!'

'We owe respect to the living!' Skribble shot back. 'And that is hardly a word one can use with regard to that old harridan, is it now, hmm?'

Milton's dark eyes glowed like coals in a furnace. 'With this child's help, my lady's condition is soon to be reversed,' he said softly. Then he stood aside, to reveal a statue behind him, blocking the doorway from the octagonal chamber.

It was the statue of the sad woman that had been placed outside the workshop. As she took in the crisp lines of the pristine white creation, Milly gasped in fear.

The statue was sad no longer. The stone woman was smiling.

Still roaming the rambling corridors of Milton's house, Jess, Jason and Michael were no longer creeping about. Now they were clomping here and there, opening and slamming doors, growing more and more agitated. *I want someone to hear us now,* Jess thought to herself. *Mr Milton's nice, he won't get angry—*

'Hang on, look!' said Michael with some relief, pointing ahead of them. 'It's that croc again! We must have come this way!'

Jess frowned. At the end of the silent corridor she could see it was indeed the same stuffed crocodile in a glass case they had passed before.

'Hang on, though,' said Jason nervously. 'Before, it was tucked away in a corner – not lying in the middle of the floor.'

'Someone's moved it,' Jess agreed, approaching it cautiously. Then suddenly she remembered the whispered words they'd heard on the blustery peak and held very, very still. 'Jason, Michael,' she whispered. 'The warnings we heard on the wind at the glacier – the voice said we should beware false lines on parchment.'

Jason gasped. 'You . . . you think it was talking about the lines on the map?'

'What else did it say?' asked Michael.

Chills coiled around Jess's backbone as she stared at the crocodile in the case with its cold, beady gaze and remembered the unearthly mutterings: '*Beware eyes behind glass . . .*'

She caught a flicker of movement from within the cabinet.

The crocodile had blinked.

The next moment, the glass cabinet shattered as the green, sinewy reptile burst forward towards them. Jess and Michael both yelled, but Jason was too scared to do even that. He turned on his heel and led the charge back down the corridor away from the crocodile.

'This can't be happening,' he babbled; 'it's impossible!'

'It's magic,' Michael corrected him.

The three of them ran on in blind panic through the seemingly endless passageways until Jason suddenly skidded to a halt. He could hear a slow, rhythmic *thump-thump-thump* coming from the shadowy corridor ahead of them.

Jess stopped running and clutched hold of her brother's arm. 'What's that?'

Jason seemed speechless with fright; but the next moment Jess had her impossible answer. The shabby fairground horse they'd seen earlier was somehow dragging itself towards them, animated by some unseen force to block their escape. Its painted features were jolly and bright, but its glass eyes were cold and dark.

Jess bit her lip. 'We're dreaming. This is like something from a bad horror film.'

The crocodile came crawling into sight. Its movements were stiff. Its stuffed jaws opened and shut of their own accord, the eyes glowing yellow like torch-beams, ivory teeth scraping and snapping together.

'Trapped between a stuffed croc and Muffin the Mule,' Michael groaned.

Jason spotted a wooden door to their left. 'Quick, through here!' he shouted. The door flew open at his touch.

It was then that he realized this was the same door that had almost closed on them before. He froze in the doorway, opened his mouth to shout a warning – but Michael and Jess were right behind him and bundled him through . . .

The floor disappeared beneath them into golden flashes of sputtering light.

Falling and shouting in slow motion, Michael, Jess and Jason were swallowed up by an impossible blackness.

Chapter Twenty-Two

In the octagonal chamber, Milly was still staring in horror at the stone woman with her deathly smile. 'You mean . . . *that* is your wife?'

'That is my beautiful, beloved Ayeshaka, turned to stone.' Milton reverently stroked a perfect white arm with the tips of his fingers. 'A great jest of the Genie Council.'

Skribble nodded. 'I heard the story at my mother's knee. The Council decreed that as Ayeshaka's evil heart was clearly as hard as stone, the rest of her should be made to match it. Miltakbar was sent with her to the land of mortals, to attend his queen and reflect on their folly until the end of time.'

'I reflected, all right,' Milton declared. 'I moved between the continents, steeping myself in dark wisdom. And I began to form a plan . . .'

Milly's heart quickened to hear the faint

echoes of hoarse, panic-stricken cries. 'That's my brothers and sister!' she cried. 'What's happening to them? What?'

'About time too.' Milton reached out his hand upwards, as if plucking invisible fruits from the air. With the first gesture, Jess appeared, hanging limply in the air like an abandoned marionette, her feet a few centimetres from the floor. Milly gasped, and did so again as, with a second gesture, Jason appeared beside her. With a third stab of the air, Michael shimmered into view, his dark hair flopping forward over his face.

Milly looked at Milton in awe. 'How did you bring them here?'

He smiled and opened his palm. A small golden feather lay there.

'Phoenix magic?' Milly breathed. 'The same way *we've* been travelling.'

'Alas, I have merely mastered the migration of objects through space, not through time,' Milton admitted. 'Nevertheless, for a mortal such powers are impressive, no?'

Milly stared at Jess, Jason and Michael. 'What have you done to them? Make them wake up, NOW!'

Even as she spoke, Michael twitched in mid air. 'Oh, my head,' he groaned. 'Did an elephant sit on it, or what?'

Jess stretched as if waking from a deep sleep. 'No, you've always looked like that.'

Jason stirred too, opened his eyes – and did a double take. 'Whoa! Skribble? Milly? Fenella?' He blinked several times. 'Am I dreaming?'

'Oh, Fenella!' Jess cried, seeing the bird. 'Thank goodness you're all right . . .'

'Be silent,' Milton snarled, and at his voice, Jess and Michael shook themselves properly awake.

'OK, this is not good,' said Michael, clocking the scene in front of him. 'So that's where the statue went. Any chance I could go home and hide under the bed?'

'I hope my little pets upstairs didn't alarm you too much as they herded you along,' said Milton. 'But I did so want you to join us.'

'And you wanted them to see your power,' Milly said coldly. 'Or you'd have just got Skribble to wish them here.'

Mr Milton gave her a malicious smile. 'How clever you are, my dear.'

'Mr Milton,' said Jess in a shaky voice, 'what . . . I mean, how . . . I mean, why—'

'Worm,' Milton interrupted, turning to Skribble. 'I command you to apprise these brats of the situation without need of tedious repeated explanation.'

'Very well,' muttered Skribble, closing his

eyes and swaying on his little cloud. Lightning flashes suddenly sparked about Michael's, Jess's and Jason's heads. The three of them looked at each other in a daze.

Then Jess covered her face with her hands. 'We've been such idiots!'

Jason stared at Milton. 'So *you* were the one Skribble warned us about!'

'But we thought it was the other bloke!' Michael shook his head. 'Who's he then?'

'I know nothing of any "other bloke",' said Milton dismissively. 'Now, be silent, and know that you are privileged to participate in the final stages of my master plan. I have need of all four children – according to the true prophecy of the phoenix egg.'

'What does he mean . . . ?' Fenella struggled up weakly and stared at Milton. 'What true prophecy? What do you . . . know about my egg . . . ?'

'A very good deal,' Milton informed her. 'Considering it was I who stole the first one you laid, as well as the second.'

Fenella went rigid. 'You never did! You're lying.'

'I'm afraid he is not,' said Skribble heavily.

Milton turned to a large chest on the workbench behind him and opened its lid. Inside was the spiky nest Fenella had built, spun through with gold, the sticks daubed with ash, flecks of silphium scattered inside like strange petals. 'You should thank me,' he said. 'There is and has always been only one Phoenix in existence. Had the egg hatched, it might have marked an end to your own life as the new hatchling took your place.'

Milly gasped. 'Is that true, Skribble?'

'I do not know,' Skribble admitted. 'A phoenix egg is a mystery, a paradox, it is something that shouldn't be. Miltakbar is right that there is just one phoenix. She is unique. There isn't a scholar alive in this world or the Realm of Genies who truly understands what will happen if the phoenix hatches an egg. She is reborn from ashes so what need does she have of an egg?'

'For the hope it brings,' Fenella whispered, closing her eyes. 'The promise of someone to love and cherish for ever.'

'Such a promise was taken from me,' Milton hissed. 'Why should I not take it from you? And yes, the egg might be a paradox but there is one thing all agree upon – it contains mighty powers that can be unlocked and used. Powers of rebirth and renewal unheard of in all history.'

'*Rebirth!*' Michael suddenly got it. 'So that's what you're doing! You want to use Fenella's egg to bring your missus back to life! I bet that's why you took her egg the first time too.'

'Yes,' Milton snarled. 'But agents of the Genie Council saw fit to track me down to Cairo and halt my work. To teach me a lesson they imprisoned me in a pyramid for fifty years . . . But the fates smiled on me. For there, on my doorstep, I found the Brothers of the Sun Bird.'

Jason's eyes were saucer-wide. 'That cult we ran into? You met them too?'

'A most knowledgeable clan,' said Milton. 'I traded some of my dark secrets for many of theirs.' He nodded, a gleam in his eyes. 'Writing with ink made from the magic-infused ashes of the phoenix nest, using magical feathers shed when *you*, Michael, hurled that stone at Fenella's head, the Sun-Bird priest wrote prophecies that truly came to pass.'

Michael hung his head. 'I'm sorry, everyone.'

'None of us could have known,' Jess told him.

'Just as none of you could have known of the prophecy I had discovered,' hissed Milton. 'It concerned the power of the phoenix egg. It spoke of how the egg's powers would be unlocked with four magical ingredients and used to bring a long dead soul to life.'

'Four ingredients,' echoed Jess.

'Don't tell us,' groaned Michael. 'Gold spun from tomorrow's sunlight, phoenix nest ashes, a dewdrop from Mount Thingummy—'

'And silphium leaves,' Jason concluded.

Fenella gasped. 'So those ingredients weren't needed to help my egg to hatch.'

'Just to help *you* to use the egg to bring your stone bride back to life,' said Milly.

'Quite right.' Milton smiled craftily. 'And so I used you children to collect the ingredients on my behalf, with that magical map the worm crafted for me.'

'But why get us to do it?' Michael demanded. 'You had Skribble, surely he could have whipped up those ingredients in a flash?'

'No.' Skribble shook his head. 'The Genie Council knew of the prophecy, you see, and protected the ingredients with a charm that stopped any genie from touching them or collecting them by magic.'

'And so I needed humans,' said Milton. 'More particularly, I needed the four of *you*. For once you travelled back in time and met the Brothers of the Sun Bird, you became a *part* of the priest's prophecies! They wrote about you and the role you would play in unleashing the power of the egg – four children who balanced selflessness with greed . . . Who risked all for the phoenix and partook of her sacred charms and powers.' He pointed at Michael. 'The boy who would buy respect with gold.' He stabbed a finger at Jess. 'The girl who feared failure and tasted ash.' He sneered at Jason. 'The ungainly lad who fed on herbs of antiquity in the hope he might learn to belong. And the little girl . . .'

'But I haven't done anything,' Milly protested.

'Not yet,' Milton agreed. 'But it was written that you would succumb to temptation like your siblings, that you would taste the dewdrop. And so, for the charm to work, you *must* taste of it.'

'I shan't,' said Milly. 'I'm not letting your stupid, horrible charm come true. You can shove your dewdrop down your pants!'

'Ridiculous child, you cannot thwart my will!' Milton loomed over her. 'Why do you think I lured away your siblings so that you, youngest and most helpless, might come to my sanctum alone?' He chuckled. 'I cast a spell of obedience here ahead of your arrival – and it has now had time to work upon you.'

'No!' Milly shouted. 'There's no spell on me, you're—'

'Be silent and hold still!' The old man snapped his fingers.

Milly's voice choked away. Her eyes widened with fear, and she looked helplessly at Skribble. A tiny tear was trickling down the worm's crinkly cheek.

'You *shall* taste the dewdrop,' Milton assured her, 'just as your siblings will play their part in the ceremony.'

'You haven't charmed *us*,' said Michael shakily. 'How come? Not up to it?'

'It is not necessary,' Milton informed him smugly. 'Disobey me and young Milly here shall regret it.'

Fenella raised her head wearily, trembling with rage. 'I'm at the end of my life now, Miltakbar,' she croaked. 'But if you harm these children, I swear to you that when I come back reborn you'll regret what you've done for ever.'

'There'll be no chance of you coming back this time, phoenix,' Milton sneered. He looked at Jason. 'Now, boy. I know you carry the drop of dew.' Milton snapped his fingers. 'Give it to me.'

'Um . . . OK.' Milly saw a strange almost furtive look cross Jason's face as he swallowed hard and reached into his trouser pocket. 'Now, where did I put it . . . ?'

Milly strained against the spell, desperate to escape. But it was no good, she couldn't move a muscle. Through the window, she could just see the statue of the fighting gryphons. *Nothing like the real thing*, she thought, picturing George and the way he had smiled at her . . .

Suddenly the sun came out, shining through the window, and something on her anorak glinted in the light. It was her zip. Where George's blade-like claws had swiped her coat to get at the gold, he had cut clean through the metal fastener. Now the torn and toothy metal was gleaming like it was made of gold itself. But why?

'Hurry, boy,' snarled Milton, advancing on Jason. 'Or I'll take the damnable dewdrop by force!'

'It's here,' said Jason shakily, handing over a small plastic tube with a pipette inside. 'Take it.'

'No, Jase!' cried Michael.

'He has chosen wisely.' The old man turned to face Milly and removed the red stopper from the tube. 'Now, take the pipette and drink . . .'

Milly couldn't stop her right arm from rising, reaching for the pipette. A laugh of triumph escaped Milton's lips.

'Wait!' cried Skribble. 'First, have the child take off that raggedy old coat. This is a moment of great ceremony and import, Miltakbar, have you no sense of occasion?'

Michael groaned. 'I actually thought the worm was gonna help for a minute!'

'Do as the worm suggests, girl,' rasped Milton.

Milly shrugged off the anorak and placed it in a heap beside Fenella on the table.

'Now, drink!'

Milly could hardly see through tears; her hand jerked closer to the tube and she took out the pipette.

'No, Mil!' Michael urged her.

I can't stop, she thought, closing her eyes and taking a deep breath as she raised the pipette to her lips . . .

Chapter Twenty-Three

Michael stared helplessly as his sister pressed her tongue to the glass pipette and squeezed the rubber tip. He was almost grateful when Milton, crowing with laughter, swept in front of him and blocked his view.

'And so the thousand-year prophecy is complete,' the old man cried. 'At last, the ritual can begin – and my long life's work be completed.'

'Evil such as yours shall never prosper!' cried Skribble fiercely.

'Enough, worm,' Milton commanded. 'You are my slave. Summon the symbols of power for the ritual as I have revealed them to you.'

'As you will it, so shall it be,' Skribble muttered. Michael noticed him hop from his little cloud onto the torn material of Milly's anorak. He raised his small, segmented body up into the air and started to wail and wriggle. '*Nemedi omnes, astram incarnate . . .*'

A shiver ran through Michael as mysterious squiggles in blackest ink appeared over the white tiled floor of the octagonal room, their patterns uniting in two interlocking circles. Milton tenderly reached out both arms to the statue of his bride Ayeshaka and closed one fist about a golden feather in his hand. The air seemed to shimmer as the statue reappeared beside him in the dead centre of one of the circles. Milton lifted the phoenix nest from the workbench and placed it reverently at the feet of his beloved. The large, heavy egg inside seemed almost aglow with golden light.

Skribble stopped chanting, but continued to wriggle on top of the anorak.

'Now, children,' hissed Milton. 'You must take your places for the ceremony.'

'Get stuffed,' Michael retorted.

'Perhaps it is the phoenix I shall stuff.' He smiled. 'After all, a feeble bird, manacled to the table, can put up so little resistance . . .'

The skies were darkening through the eight windows. The black markings began to glow.

Milton turned to Michael, Jason and Jess. 'Stand in the second circle,' he commanded. 'Place your hands against the stone flesh of Ayeshaka. Your humanity will soften her heart so that the magical essences of the egg may touch the core of her being . . .'

Michael and Jess each took a hold of one of the statue's hands. Jason and Milly were directed by Milton to press their hands against the statue's feet. Filled with fear and sorrow, Michael looked at his sister's head. He hated being so powerless, hated that she'd taken the dewdrop . . .

Milton lowered the phoenix egg back into the nest. He rubbed the silphium leaves against the gleaming shell, daubed a single, strange symbol there in ash and pressed his fingers against the threads of gold that bound the twigs together.

Suddenly Fenella burst into noisy sobs, and Skribble joined in. He hopped off the anorak and clung to her manacled leg.

'Be silent, fools!' Milton rasped, his eyes shining. 'The great moment is finally upon us . . .'

Dark storm clouds had rolled across the evening sky, reducing the sun to a red, warning glow. Michael could feel something like static in the air, prickling the hairs on the back of his neck. Kneeling between the nest and his stony queen, Milton began to chant secret words under his breath. Within seconds, curls of strangely scented smoke began to rise up from the phoenix egg and the statue became suffused with light.

To Michael's horror, he realized that the cold, white stone beneath his fingers was starting to soften, turning clay-grey and clammy . . .

Jason cringed. 'Her feet just twitched!'

'Something's wrong,' hissed Milton. 'She should have returned to flesh and blood at once. What is happening?' He stared up at the pale, glowing figure in rapture. 'Come back to me, my queen! My old heart is yours. The strength and purity of youth is yours. The powers of magical rebirth are yours—'

'AND SO ARE MY CLAWS, YOU OLD BAG!' yelled Fenella, launching herself into the air. Her talons raked at the glowing statue's face and neck, showering Milly, Jason and Milton with crumbling chunks of stone. Milton screamed with anger – and Milly elbowed him in the ribs as hard as she could. He lost his balance and fell out of the circle.

'Let go of the statue, children!' cried Skribble.

Michael jumped away but Jess couldn't move. 'This thing's holding on to me!' she shrieked. 'She's got my fingers!'

Fenella flapped down and brought her sharp beak down hard on the statue's wrist. The stony fingers flexed and spasmed. Jess yanked her hand free and leaped out of the circle.

'No!' shouted Milton, on his knees.

'*Yes*, prune features!' Michael yelled, grabbing Milly's old anorak from the table and hurling it into Milton's face. As he did so, Fenella swooped down on top of the evil magician and knocked him sprawling.

'The egg,' Jess muttered, looking at the smoking nest still in the magic circle. She tried to drag it clear. 'Michael, help me!' she shouted.

Michael knelt beside her and together they tugged on the hot, sharp sticks with all their strength. The nest began to move. 'Jase, Milly, come on!'

Milly and Jason yanked at the heavy nest too. Even Skribble whooshed down on his little cloud and added his strength to the struggle. 'It's moving,' Michael shouted. 'Just a little more . . .'

'Scatter, loveys!' yelled Fenella, leaving Milton and aiming straight for the spiky bundle. Jess, Michael and the others scrambled back as she hurled herself against the side of the nest. In an explosion of twigs, the nest and the glowing egg inside it were pushed clear of the darkly shining symbols.

Milton screamed in horror as the glow about

the statue began to fade and the grey skin faded into chalk-white once more. 'It cannot be!' he croaked. 'I cannot lose now after so long!'

'I reckon you just have!' Michael shouted back.

'Ayeshaka!' Milton wailed, his hat askew, fiercely embracing the statue, tears pouring from his eyes as he stared up at her ruined face. 'Sweet Ayeshaka, it was my wish – my only wish – to stand by your side for ever!'

'*Your wish is granted!*' cried Skribble in triumph.

There was a flash of white light that made Michael shield his eyes. And when he looked again, there was no longer one statue standing in the circle of fading symbols, but two. Milton himself was turned to stone, arms clamped tight around his beloved, gazing up at her with sightless marble eyes.

Skribble nodded to himself and let out a great sigh of relief. 'Now, you shall most certainly stand by her side,' he murmured. 'For ever.'

For a few moments, everyone stared in a dulled, dazed silence. Then Michael looked down at the nest and gasped. 'Fenella!' The bird's pale body lay sprawled on the floor.

Jess and Milly scooped up the phoenix and placed her gently on the tabletop beside the discarded chain and manacle. The bird's eyes were closed and she was barely breathing.

'She looked so weak even *before* she started chucking herself about,' said Jason.

'Her egg was at risk, and we were all in danger,' said Skribble gravely. 'So, with the last of her strength . . .'

'No, not the last.' Michael shook his head. 'It can't be the last!' He tried to swallow down the lump in his throat. 'How did she get free, anyway?'

'The sheared-through zip on Milly's anorak,' said Skribble impatiently. 'I noticed it gleam in the sunlight, and realized I could use its tip to pick the lock on Fenella's manacles.'

'It was George, Fenella!' Milly whispered to the prone phoenix. 'You've *got* to wake up, because his smile really did bring us luck, just as you said.' She couldn't hold back the tears any longer, and heavy drops splashed down onto the phoenix's mottled breast. 'You've just got to wake up.'

'The egg,' Jess breathed, pointing down at the damaged nest. 'Fenella, your egg . . .'

Michael took an involuntary step away. The large egg was pulsing blood-red, agleam and alive with unknowable energy. The sooty symbol daubed on its side burned off in colourless flames.

Fenella's eyes flickered open. 'My . . . egg?'

'Yes!' Michael felt overwhelmed by relief. 'You can't give up now, your egg needs you!'

'No good now, pet,' the bird whispered. 'Egg's ruined . . . by that old windbag's ritual . . .'

'But it *isn't* ruined,' Milly insisted. 'The ritual would never have worked properly – thanks to Jason!'

Jason smiled bashfully.

Michael frowned. 'What are you on about?'

'I never drank that dewdrop!' Milly told him.

'But we saw you,' said Jess.

'No. Like Mr Milton, you only *thought* you did!' Jason reached into his pocket and pulled out another pipette in a small glass tube – this one with a yellow stopper. 'I took two of these with me to Mount Quamquangle, so if I messed up the first time, I still had another chance.'

Milly nodded happily. 'When there was no water inside at all, I realized what Jase must have done . . .'

'But luckily Milton didn't!' Jess added, hugging her brother.

'Neither did I.' Michael wiped his brow. 'Must be why his old missus didn't come straight back to life as planned – he was a magic ingredient short!'

Fenella propped herself up on one wing. 'Then . . . I might still have a chance?'

'There's always hope,' said Skribble. 'Though today we live in shadow, tomorrow we may find the sun.'

'The sun,' Fenella cooed, a faint smile on her beak. 'Oh, I can feel its rays on my skin . . . ooooh, that's nice . . . oooooooh, it tickles . . .'

'There's no sun now, Fenella.' Michael bit his lip. 'She's gone funny.'

'No!' Skribble backed away. 'She's getting hotter.'

'She's starting to smoke!' Milly gasped. 'Fenella? Are you OK?'

Fenella struggled up with a brave smile. 'It's my time, lovey.' She winced. 'The time . . . of my new becoming.'

Jess pointed in alarm. 'And your egg is going crazy, Fenella!' It looked more like a giant ruby now, flaming with power.

'We've got to get her to the nest!' Michael said anxiously.

'I can make it.' Fenella was panting for breath. 'I can make it, but . . . I don't know if I can hatch an egg. It's never been done before, and look at me, I'm a mess.'

'No. Never.' Milly blew a kiss down at her. 'You're fantastic.'

'We all think so,' said Jess quietly. Jason nodded, and even Skribble inclined his head.

'I don't do mush,' said Michael firmly as he crouched beside the rumpled bird. 'But, look, Fenella . . .' He gazed into her dim blue eyes. 'If anyone can do this, you can.'

'We believe in you,' said Milly fervently.

'Then, I suppose it's time I believed in myself!' Fenella smiled up at them. 'Be seeing you, lovies.' She closed her eyes tightly, and rolled off the stone slab she lay on. She fell briefly through the air and landed on top of the egg.

The second she touched it, Fenella burst into flames.

'Fenella!' Milly screamed.

Skribble zoomed about on his little cloud. 'Back, children!' he shouted as both egg and phoenix were lost in a fierce crimson blaze.

Michael shook his head. 'But we can't leave her.'

'We must!' said Skribble firmly.

Jason coughed on the smoke. 'Quick, let's get out through one of these windows!' He pushed past the embracing statues, jumped clumsily up onto the workbench and tugged at the window handles. 'I can't do it,' he cried. 'The silphium must have worn off!'

'Get out of the way then.' Michael climbed

onto the workbench beside him, forced open one of the leaded glass windows and then he and the others scrambled through. Thick broiling clouds of smoke chased them outside, all the way to the statue of the gryphons. They sheltered behind it, watching as the smoke-plumes rose up over the roof of the octagonal chamber and faded to nothing.

Michael looked at Jess. 'Any words of phoenix wisdom to give us comfort then?'

'No,' Jess said, staring into space. 'Her voice has gone.'

They waited tensely; the children huddling together, the bookworm bobbing about on his cloud. Daylight ebbed away into the deep indigo of a summer evening. And at last, the smoke from inside Milton's building died away to nothing.

'Fenella?' called Jess uncertainly.

Gesturing that the others should keep back, Michael crossed to the little building. There were no choking fumes, no sign of damage at all. The statues of Milton and Ayeshaka still loomed silently inside, like memories of evil.

But where Fenella's nest had been, there lay only a pile of charred sticks covered with ash, and the egg, unhatched and blackened. Nothing more.

Michael turned back to the others, numb

and uncomprehending, and his voice when it came was the smallest thing in the world.

'Fenella didn't make it,' he said.

The children all stared at the burned nest.

'It was all for nothing,' Jess whispered. 'The egg didn't hatch. Fenella's gone.'

Milly went over to the egg and warily touched it. 'It's cold. Like stone.' She looked at Skribble, who was floating beside Jason, a confused look on his face. 'What happened?'

For once Skribble didn't try to bluster. 'I . . . I don't know.' He floated over and looked down at the egg. Milly saw him swallow before he spoke softly. 'But it appears that the world is now without a phoenix. And a much greyer place it will be as a result.'

Tears sprang to Milly's eyes as she shook her head helplessly. 'Fenella can't have gone!'

Jess put her arm around her. 'Oh, Milly.'

'It's not fair!' Jason burst out angrily.

Michael nodded. 'Life isn't fair, mate.'

'What should we do with the nest and the egg?' Milly sniffed. 'We can't just leave them here.' Her eyes flicked to the stone statue of Milton and his bride and her voice rose. 'Not with *them!*'

'Let's take the nest and the egg to the workshop for now,' Jess said quickly. 'We can decide what to do properly tomorrow.'

'I guess Michael and I have to come back here anyway,' Jason realized. 'To talk to the earlier us, and make sure that whole meeting happened.'

'I wondered why I had that look in my eye,' said Michael quietly, shaking his head. 'I thought I was just sad about the gold. As if that really matters—' He broke off. 'Come on, Jase. Give me a hand with the nest.'

Skribble was floating above the burned remains, watching their work closely. 'Be careful!' he commanded.

They lifted the nest as carefully as they could and carried it slowly out of the octagonal building, Skribble floating beside them on his cloud. Milly picked up Skribble's lamp. Hugging it closely to her for comfort, she followed with Jess.

The four of them didn't say a word as they reached the workshop and laid the nest gently down on the workbench.

'We'll see you soon,' said Jess to it, almost as if Fenella was still there.

'What will you do, Skribble?' Milly asked, putting his lamp down on the bench. 'You won't go, just yet, will you? Please say you won't.' She didn't think she could bear it if he disappeared too.

Skribble looked down at the dusty egg,

an unreadable expression on his face. 'I shall remain here tonight to watch over her.'

Jess didn't think she had ever felt so sad. 'OK, Skribble. Well, we'll come back after school tomorrow.'

Jason and Michael nodded mutely.

Milly kissed the worm on top of his head. 'See you tomorrow, Skribble.'

Jess took Milly's hand. With one last look at the cold ash-covered egg and the genie worm sitting on his cloud beside it, the children left the workshop.

Chapter Twenty-Four

Michael lingered outside the school gates, waiting for Jess to show. It had not been a top day – what he'd noticed of it, anyway. He couldn't stop thinking about the weirdness of being trapped in Milton's house, the scariness of the magic he and the others had been caught up in, and . . .

And Fenella.

Stop it, he told himself, clenching both fists. *Suicide to cry at school.*

He thought of the egg, sitting there so lost-looking in that singed and spiky nest. He barely noticed the other kids milling about him as they drifted off down the school drive. The real world seemed so pale after the wildness of the adventure he'd just lived through.

He suddenly saw Jess walking towards him. One look at her eyes and he knew she was feeling just the same.

'Thought school today would never end,' said Jess ruefully.

'Me too.' Michael glanced away. 'Not that I really want to go back to Milton's place and . . . You know.'

'It'll be good to see Skribble again, though,' said Jess, forcing some jollity into her voice.

'True,' Michael agreed. 'I just wish we didn't have to go back there to do it.'

'You and Jason need to be there to talk to the versions of us from last Saturday,' Jess reminded him. 'Did you remember to bring that T-shirt of yours?'

Michael nodded and patted his bag. 'I found it last night.' He sighed. 'You know, it's so weird, realizing I was – *I will be* – putting on such an act.'

'Speaking of acts, I said I'd go to the church hall tonight to wait for Milly. It's about the last thing I feel like doing.' Jess sighed. 'Well, apart from revising. That would be worse!'

'Jess!' A girl's voice calling to them jolted them back to reality. It was Colette, closely followed by Jess's gang of girlfriends. Michael watched them swarm up and surround Jess, ignoring him completely.

'Jess, it was like you were on another planet today.' Colette sounded full of concern. 'These exams are totally stressing you, aren't they?'

Jess opened her mouth to argue otherwise. Then, instead, she shrugged and nodded.

Colette put a hand on Jess's shoulder and grinned. 'Well, your friends are coming to the rescue!'

Jodie nodded and passed her a colourful CD case. 'I've got you a *Learn History* quick study program on CD-ROM!'

Jess looked at it, her cheeks reddening. 'Really?'

'I thought you people were her friends?' joked Michael.

'Ha, ha.' Jodie shot him a look before turning back to Jess. 'My mum says it's really good.'

'And she should know, she's a history teacher,' put in Natasha, handing Jess a small brown bottle. 'Here, I've got you some lavender oil to help you chill out while you load it up.'

'And get this,' Colette added. 'If we all pass, my mum says she'll let us have a nail painting session at the beauty salon she goes to! So – I thought we could study together all weekend at mine and then we'll be super-ready for the exam on Monday.'

Jodie nodded. 'If we're all revising together, we can test each other and we can't wimp out and watch TV instead!'

Jess grinned. 'Thanks. That would really help.'

Colette looked at her anxiously. 'Jess, you do know that even if you fail miserably and we can't be in the same lessons, you will always be our mate, don't you? Promise us you don't think anything else.'

Their eyes met. 'I promise,' said Jess, feeling a glow of happiness inside. 'Thank you.' She included the other two in her gaze. 'Thanks, all of you.'

Natasha smiled at her. 'Shut up with the thanks!'

'What are mates for?' Jodie added.

Colette grinned. 'Now are you walking home with us or not?'

'Actually, Michael and I have got stuff to do,' said Jess. 'So I can't tonight.'

'Little brother stuff, huh?' Colette gave her a sympathetic look. 'OK, see you tomorrow then.'

'See you!' Jess called, waving as they walked off.

'Little brother stuff?' Michael frowned as he watched them go. 'Even so, I wish I had mates like that,' he admitted. 'Well, you know, mates like that but more manly and cool.'

'You *have* mates,' Jess told him. 'So what if they're friends with Rick the Slick too?'

'I just can't be one of Rick's hangers-on. I can't.' Michael shrugged. 'Anyway, you'd better go home and meet Milly; she'll be wondering where you are. I told Jason to wait for me at the bottom of Flint Street so we can go through what we say to ourselves on the way to Milton's.'

'Well, take care,' said Jess. 'We never did find out about that weird bloke watching us.'

Michael shrugged. 'And we probably never will.'

'*Hey, Michael!*'

For an improbable second, Michael thought it was that very same mystery man calling his name. Then he realized it was actually Rick the Slick of all people, appearing from behind the bike sheds. No cause for alarm, but definitely cause for a quick getaway. 'I'm off,' he muttered to Jess. 'Laters.'

She waved briefly as he hurried away down the school drive.

Michael threaded a path across Moreways Meet more or less on autopilot, lost in his own thoughts, until he saw Jason at the bottom of Flint Street, slumped against the signpost with a face as long as the walk ahead to Milton's.

'All right?' said Michael.

Jason looked up and mustered a smile. 'Suppose.' Then the smile dropped and his eyes widened as he looked past Michael. 'Oh, no.'

Michael turned round – and a chill of fear went through him.

Just a few metres away stood the man with the scruffy hair and the glowering face. The man who'd watched him in the junk shop, and who'd been turning up ever since. The man Michael had decided they would never see again. *Me and my big mouth*, he thought.

The man said nothing, just went on watching with beady eyes. Michael checked behind him for other people in the street. Typically, no one was about. It was just him, Jason and this sinister stranger.

'Who are you?' Michael demanded. 'Where are you from?'

'I've been wanting to talk to you,' the man said, in a nasal, whiny sort of voice. 'I want to do a deal.'

Jason gulped. 'Are you . . . magic?'

'Magic?' The man snorted. 'What're you on about?' He stabbed a finger at Michael. 'I saw him try to palm off some gold on the geezer in the junk shop. Sounded pretty desperate. And if the junk shop doesn't want it, well . . . maybe I can help you out.'

Michael almost laughed out loud. He turned to Jason, who was looking totally startled. 'All this time we thought we were being watched by some evil, all-seeing genie or something, and it's just some dodgy old geezer!'

The man smiled, showing teeth undoubtedly

as crooked as the rest of him. 'Show me that gold, son.'

'I've changed my mind about the gold, "Dad",' said Michael coldly. 'It's not for sale.'

The man's smile dropped. 'I don't think you heard me,' he said quietly, taking a step closer to Michael and Jason. 'We're going to do a deal. And I'm making the terms.'

Michael felt a sudden wave of fury. 'Look, mate, this is not a good time to start threatening me and my brother, OK? Not after what we've been going through. So, push off. Leave us alone, or we'll . . .' He frowned, flummoxed, and looked at Jason again. 'What'll we do?'

'We'll . . .' Jason shrugged, flustered. 'We'll tell our mum and dad?'

The man seemed unimpressed. 'Look, I don't like picking on kids,' he went on in a reasonable voice, 'but I want that gold. And it can't really be yours – you just wanna get rid, don't you?' He came closer. 'If you won't sell it, maybe I'll just take it—'

'Take *this!*' yelled Jason suddenly. He hurled himself at the man, bringing him down in a perfectly timed rugby tackle. The man gave a startled gasp of surprise as he crashed to the ground.

'Nice one, Jase!' Michael cried. 'You haven't even got your powers any more!'

'I know!' Jason said, beaming with joy – for all of a single microsecond before the man grabbed hold of his wrist. Jason tried to scramble clear, but couldn't. Michael waded in and tried to wrestle Jason free, but the scruffy man grabbed his arm, clamping down hard on the skin. Michael gasped, tore himself free and managed to yank Jason away from the man too. Swearing, the man shambled back to his feet and was about to charge after Michael and Jason—

When suddenly a young, fresh-faced policeman sprinted from round the junction and grabbed hold of the dodgy man. 'All right, that's enough,' he shouted. 'Picking a fight with little kids? You should be ashamed!'

Michael's relief was such that he was prepared to let the 'little kids' reference go.

'These kids have nicked some gold,' the scruffy man whined. 'I was only trying to get it back off them.'

'We haven't stolen anything,' Jason said hotly.

'Right!' Michael agreed. He turned out his pockets – knowing the phoenix gold was back at home – and Jason quickly did the same. 'Nothing!'

'He just started threatening us!' Jason went on.

'I know,' said the copper. 'This young man

told me.' He turned and beckoned to someone behind him – and Michael gaped in amazement.

'*Rick?*' he spluttered.

Rick shrugged, a little awkwardly. 'I wanted to talk to you back at school, but you didn't hear me so I went after you. And I saw that bloke was following you too – so when I noticed the policeman, well . . .'

'He asked me to check things out.' The young constable grinned happily at the sullen, scruffy man in his grip. 'And thank God he did! I recognize this bloke from the station files in Quilborough. Petty crook. Wanted for fencing stolen property but jumped bail.'

'Is there a reward for catching him?' said Michael eagerly.

The copper smiled. 'A free tour of the police station when you come to make a statement,' he said, straight-faced. 'Meantime, I'll need your names and addresses . . .'

Jason reeled off the details while Michael eyed his watch. 'We're in a bit of rush, officer. Got an urgent appointment and time's running out. Can we, um, come by later?'

'Should be fine,' the policeman agreed happily, turning to the scruffy, scowling man. 'My first arrest! Come on then, there's a lot of people who want to talk to you . . .'

Michael breathed a sigh of relief as the cop

bundled the crook away, and looked at Rick. 'Thanks,' he said grudgingly.

'Any time,' said Rick. 'I mean, I know you two could have taken care of that bloke yourselves, but . . .' He shrugged. 'I was well impressed with the way you gave him lip, Michael. Cool. No wonder the other lads look up to you so much.'

'Huh?' Michael stared. 'They do?'

'Josh, Thomas, Sam, they're always going on about you.' Rick grinned. 'It's why I wanted to be one of your gang in the first place.'

'My gang?' Michael stared in wonder.

Rick shrugged. 'Who else's?'

Michael raised his eyebrows. 'You know, Rick, you're not as dumb as Jason looks.'

Rick grinned – then turned to Jason. 'Fair play, though – I saw your tackle, it was wicked. No wonder you took out your brother the other night.'

'Oh, we . . . we were just mucking about,' said Jason. With sudden inspiration, he went on: 'I, um, bet Michael a week of his chores that he couldn't trick you.'

'Yeah?' Rick laughed. 'Then I can see why you gave it a go, Mikey. Sneaky stepbruv you have there.' He looked at Jason again. 'You know, I heard how you caused a rumpus in the junior football tournament. And now I've seen that tackle, I'm wondering how you'd make out in rugby.'

'Rugby?' Jason repeated in a daze.

'Yeah, you've obviously got some natural talent. I could help you – train you up a bit. I'm trying to get a team together for games down the park on Saturday afternoons.' Rick shrugged. 'You could try out for us if you want.'

'Me?' Jason nodded so hard he nearly bruised his chin on his chest. 'Oh, wow! Yes, I do want!'

'Be cool, Jase,' Michael hissed. 'Well, Rick – thanks for the assist, mate, but like we told the bill, we've got to split for now. Catch you tomorrow, yeah?'

'Tomorrow, right.' Rick shook his head admiringly. 'I can't believe you're being so cool about that creep attacking you. Excellent. See ya!'

Michael knocked knuckles with him, then strode away down the street with Jason in tow. '*That* he can't believe,' he muttered. 'If we could only tell him that after all we've been through in the last few days, that scrawny old fence means next to nothing!'

'That's magic for you,' Jason murmured. 'And I think it must be magic that made Rick want me to be on his rugby team.'

'Nah,' Michael told him, clapping him hard on the back as they walked on together. 'That was just you.'

Milly was sitting alone at home, brooding. But for all her sadness, there was some niggling distraction at the back of her head, a feeling that she was missing something.

Suddenly it leaped into her head.

Way back – before we went into the future – Fenella said we couldn't go forward past her next rebirth. Now we know she wasn't reborn . . . but we still went forward into today.

Milly gasped and jumped up. 'How could we have done that if Fenella's really dead?' Then her heart sank again. *I suppose the future's been changed*, she thought. *Skribble said it could be . . .*

The thoughts kept chasing themselves around her head. And though she was supposed to wait for Jess to come and collect her, she decided she just had to talk to Skribble about things ahead of her audition. She wrote a quick note to Jess and hurried out of the door.

Auditions, she thought as she strode away. *Ha!* An image of her sobbing on Jess's shoulder flashed back into her mind. What was the point in even trying to perform? She knew she didn't get the part. But then she *had* to go, didn't she? If she didn't, the future would be wrong . . . like it already was. Unless somehow, Fenella was still alive . . .

Oh, it was all so confusing. She broke into a run.

When she reached the workshop, Skribble was floating around on his pink cloud just above the kiln. He was peering down at the blackened egg in the nest, a thoughtful expression on his face. He jumped as the door burst open. 'Ah. It's you, Milly.'

'Hi, Skribble.' As Milly looked at the egg still lying there surrounded by Fenella's ashes, a wave of intense sadness crashed over her. Her hopes quickly crumbled. The phoenix really *had* gone. She'd never see her again. 'I really miss Fenella,' she whispered.

'Mmm.' Skribble frowned and then cleared his throat. 'Where are the others? Are they coming?'

'They'll be here soon, I'm sure. I came on ahead because I wanted to talk to you.' The words suddenly burst out of Milly. 'Oh, Skribble! I don't want to go to the auditions! It's going to be awful. I know I'm going to fail and not get the part.'

'Milly, Milly,' said Skribble, shaking his head. 'Have your adventures with magic really taught you nothing? Surely you know that we can always fashion our own fate.'

'But I saw what will happen, Skribble,' Milly protested. 'Although I don't know how, because I thought we couldn't use Fenella's feather to travel forward to a time after she . . . you know.'

Then she noticed the golden feather Mr Milton had used was lying beside the kiln. 'Oh,' she sighed. 'Maybe it happened because *that's* still here.'

'Travelling into the future is an unpredictable business, my girl. The truth of things can often be deceptive. Very deceptive indeed.' Skribble's eyes swivelled round to the egg and a smile creased his face. 'For instance . . .'

Milly followed his gaze and gasped. Strands of smoke had appeared from nowhere, wreathing around the golden egg and the ash.

'What's happening?' she breathed.

'I dared to hope . . .' Skribble scowled and shook his head. 'No, I dared to *believe* that—'

The egg rumbled and shook.

'Back, Milly!' the bookworm genie commanded. 'Get back from the nest!' He zoomed to the far side of the workshop on his cloud.

Milly ran after him. 'What's going on?'

'The egg's about to hatch!' declared Skribble.

'Hatch!' Milly echoed in astonishment. 'But . . . but how? Why?'

Skribble gave no answer as the egg began to grow. Smoke curled around the shell, growing thicker and thicker.

'Come on,' breathed Skribble. 'You can do it, my dear! Of course you can!'

Suddenly the whole nest seemed to explode

in flames. A curtain of fire whooshed upwards to the ceiling. Milly gasped and shrank back, putting her hands up to shield herself from the burning heat.

CRACK!

The loud splitting noise ripped through the air – followed by a joyful whooping cry. The next second, a golden bird had shot out of the top of the flames, turning a somersault in the air, the tip of every golden feather ablaze.

'Fenella!' cried Milly. But this wasn't the Fenella she had last seen. This was a new, slim and slinky Fenella! Her feathers were long, lustrous and golden. Her blue eyes danced and shimmered like the clearest, deepest seas. But when the phoenix spoke, there was no mistaking her.

'Milly, love! I'm back! Ooooh, look at your shocked little duckling face. Did you imagine I was gone for ever? Not me!' The phoenix whizzed in a mad circle around the workshop. 'You can't keep a good bird down! So how are my hips? Do they look big with these new feathers? Oooh, where's a mirror, where's . . . Hey, look!' she shrieked, spotting the worm on his cloud next to Milly. 'There's Skribble! Why . . .' Her voice grew flirtatious as she landed on the window ledge next to his cloud and put her head on one side. 'Hello there, you goooorgeous little worm!' She fluttered her eyelashes at him.

Skribble looked flustered. 'Um . . . good day to you too, Fenella. You are to be congratulated on a feat of quite startling endurance.'

Fenella gave him a playful little nudge with her beak. 'Waiting up for me, were you? You wicked little devil! Oooh, yes, I know your sort!'

Milly's heart felt close to bursting. 'But Fenella,' she said, 'we thought you'd died!'

'Not me, duckling!' she chuckled. 'The rebirth from the ashes just took a little longer this time, that's all. It was the chicks! They must have soaked up some of my magic, greedy little beggars, delayed my coming back!'

'Chicks?' Milly repeated, not sure if she'd heard right.

Fenella flew to the nest. The flames were slowly dying down. She fanned away the smoke with her wings. 'Just look at them!' she cried. 'A clutch of four! Did you ever hear of such a thing in all your born days!'

'Oh, wow . . .' Milly stared. As the smoke cleared she saw that there, in the nest, were four small round phoenixes surrounded by the last few flickering flames! Their feathers were fluffy and their blue eyes were huge.

'Two girls, two boys!' Fenella said proudly, nuzzling the nearest chick with her beak.

'But . . .' Milly turned to Skribble. 'How?'

'Oh, yes, Skribble, lovey!' Fenella looked at him expectantly. 'Explain, please, do.'

'Ah yes, well . . . hmm . . .' Skribble began. 'Well, it's my belief that although the gathered ingredients were not actually needed for the hatching, they all contained magic. Given that they surrounded the egg – and that four somewhat magical children were feeding energy into it as well – the magic potential of the egg was actually increased. The energies of rebirth lingered on, and instead of one chick, four appeared. Four with rather different qualities, it would appear!'

Following his gaze, Milly realized that one of the chicks was turning rapid somersaults, another was trilling a beautiful song, the third was preening its incredibly beautiful golden feathers and the fourth was simply looking around with a very wise expression and nodding as if agreeing with a voice in its little head.

'Then we might have helped?' Milly squealed. 'Really?'

'I'm sure of it!' Fenella smiled happily. 'Oh, Skribble, is there anyone alive more clever than you?'

Milly saw Skribble's mouth begin to twitch into a smile. But then he coughed and hastily assumed his usual grumpy expression.

The chicks began to cheep and open their mouths. 'Listen to the little dears,' Fenella clucked. 'I'd better get looking for some grub for them.' She glanced around. 'Where are the others then, Milly, lovey?' She looked suddenly worried. 'I hope nothing's happened to them. They are OK, aren't they?'

'Yes,' Milly said quickly. 'They'll be here soon. I just came on ahead because I wanted to talk to Skribble.' She remembered about the auditions and glanced at her watch. 'Oh, no! The auditions will be about to start. What should I do, Skribble?'

'Go, Milly. The future is not to be feared but to be faced. Remember the words of my map – *know yourself, trust yourself, believe in yourself.*' He glanced at Fenella and the chicks. 'And believe in magic! Sometimes the most miraculous things happen when we least expect it.'

'Too right, lovey. It's never too late for a comeback!' Fenella fluttered over. 'You know what the ancients of Mount Quamquangle used to say – "Every day we must forget what we know and learn it afresh." And I know what they mean – just look at me with four scrumptious chicks. Who'd ever have thought it?' She laughed. 'No one really knows what the future holds. How boring would it be if you did? Just go into that audition room and do your best. Whatever happens, if you do that, you'll be able to hold your head up high.'

Milly looked from Fenella to Skribble, starting to smile. 'OK,' she said. 'I'll go!'

Skribble smiled while Fenella whooped and turned a loop-the-loop. 'You go, my lovely! Go and sing your heart out for me – and for my chicks!'

Milly felt determination flood through her.

'I will,' she declared. 'Whatever happens, I really will!'

Just as Milly reached the church hall, she saw the boys coming up the road. 'Where've you been? We've got so much to tell you!' said Jason, running up to her.

'Not as much as I've got to tell you,' Milly panted. 'But first I've got my audition!'

'I know,' said Jess, appearing from across the road. 'I've been waiting for you at the hall. You shouldn't have left without me, I was worried that weird watching man had got you.'

'He tried to get me and Jase,' said Michael.

Jess stared. 'He what?'

'It's OK, he's been arrested now and we're fine.' Jason beamed. 'Better than fine.'

Better than you can know, thought Milly, biting back a smile. She was about to blurt out what had happened when Jess yanked hold of her hand and started to drag her away. 'Come *on*, Milly. We can all catch up later – you're going to miss your spot.'

'And *we're* gonna miss seeing ourselves,' Michael added, checking his watch. 'Come on, Jase.'

'Just *don't* go into the workshop!' Milly called to them. She wanted to be there when they saw the chicks for the first time. 'Promise me you'll wait until after my auditions. Promise!'

'Whatever, weirdo,' Michael called back, but Jason nodded kindly.

'Now get your butt into that audition.' Jess gave Milly a kiss on the cheek. 'Little orphan Annie!'

Taking a deep breath, Milly hurried inside.

Jess sat down on the wall and waited anxiously. The minutes dragged by. She wondered how Jason and Michael were doing, meeting themselves from a few days ago, and how Milly was getting on inside the church hall. It felt so strange, something so magical and something so ordinary happening around her at the same time.

At long last, the doors opened and people started to come out. Jess saw Milly standing on the top of the steps, tears glistening in her eyes, looking stunned and pale.

'Well, Milly?' Jess called uncertainly.

Milly met her eyes and ran down the steps. 'Jess!' she gasped, flinging herself into her stepsister's arms. 'Oh, Jess!'

'Hey!' Jess murmured soothingly, her heart sinking. 'Oh, Milly. I'm sorry but there will be other plays, other parts . . .'

'No!' Milly said, half sobbing in astonishment and relief. 'You don't understand! I'm only crying because I can't believe it! I *got* the part, Jess – I'm Annie!'

'Oh, wow!' Jess hugged her tight. 'That's amazing! Your dream come true!'

Milly pulled suddenly away. Her eyes flicked to the gateway where she'd stood and watched this very scene all those crazy days ago. She thought she saw someone running away up the road towards Mr Milton's house. *Me*, she thought. *I saw this but I didn't know what I'd really seen . . . Just as none of us knew what we were seeing when Fenella . . .*

'Come on.' Now it was Milly's turn to haul Jess away. 'The boys will have finished by now.'

'They're going to wait for us in the gardens,' said Jess, frowning. 'But I don't see what's the hurry—'

'You will!'

They ran up the road and down the driveway that led to Mr Milton's house. Milly ran even faster as she spotted Jason and Michael making for the workshop.

'There you are!' Michael said as they arrived. 'We got fed up waiting. You know, it was SO weird hanging about in Milton's creepy house for the younger us to turn up, but we couldn't risk being spotted . . .' He scanned Milly's face. 'How did it go?'

'I got the part!' cried Milly. 'I'm Annie!'

'Brilliant!' exclaimed Jason.

Michael groaned. 'So now we have to listen to you singing all day and all night.' Just as she was about to thump him, he grinned. 'Nice one, Mil!'

'And you did it without any magic help,' said Jason.

'Probably *because* you didn't have any magic help,' Michael suggested.

'Speaking of magic help . . .' Milly threw open the door to the workshop dramatically. 'Look inside!'

Jess, Michael and Jason stared. The sound of their collective jaws dropping was almost audible.

There was Fenella, perched on the work-bench, feeding earthworms to the tiny balls of golden fluff that were her chicks. Skribble was floating a little way off on a cloud, looking slightly worried as the phoenix chicks cheeped and opened their beaks wide and Fenella dropped the worms inside. 'There we are, yum, yum, yum.' She looked over at Milly and winked. 'Aha, here she is, back again already. Congratulations, pet! We *knew* you'd do it.'

'*I* didn't,' Milly admitted, smiling at her and Skribble. 'Oh, thank you for making me go.'

'F-F-Fenella!' stammered Jason. 'Is that you?'

Michael's eyes were goggling. 'You've gone skinny!'

Fenella flapped over and gave Michael an affectionate nip on the end of his nose. 'I'd prefer *slender* or *svelte*, if you don't mind, pet!'

'But you're OK,' Jess squealed. 'And you've got chicks!'

'Four of them!' Fenella plumped up her feathers. 'What a to-do! One chick would have been quite enough for me but now I've got four to look after.' A happy smile crossed her face as one of the chicks fluttered up into the air, twittering a beautiful song. 'I'll never be lonely again!'

The chick who'd been turning somersaults before did a backward flip and almost fell out of the nest.

With a gasp, Skribble zoomed forward and nudged the chick back in.

'Thank you, Skribble, lovey,' said Fenella, unperturbed. She looked fondly round at her brood. 'Oh, I can see I'm going to have my claws and beak full with you lot.'

'So what happened, worm?' demanded Michael, still in shock. 'How come the egg hatched in the end after all?'

'Because of all that magic going on,' Milly blurted. 'Including magic from us!'

'It's certainly one for the magic vet manuals,' chortled Fenella.

'Your chicks are so cute!' said Jess admiringly.

Fenella ruffled her feathers. 'I've even thought of names for them all.' She gave the children a coy look. 'Jess, Jason, Milly and Michael,' she said, nodding to each chick in turn. 'So I shall never forget the four of you for as long as I live. And you know how long that is!'

'Cool!' said Jason, looking at the chick named after him. It rose up into the air, zoomed in a circle and turned a loop-the-loop.

Milly stroked the Milly-chick, who sang sweetly at her and rubbed her head against Milly's finger. 'Oh, Fenella, that's so sweet. Thank you!'

'It's, like, everything I ever wanted,' said Michael wryly, but there was no disguising his broad smile.

'Well, I'm afraid we're going to have to be

on our way soon, loveys,' said Fenella. 'There's places to go and things to see. A phoenix never stays in one place for long.'

'I suppose I should be on my way too,' said Skribble. 'Although I'm not sure exactly where I'm going . . .'

'Well, Skribble.' Fenella looked at him and fluttered her eyelashes. 'You could always come with us.'

Skribble hesitated.

'I'd like it *very* much,' Fenella said softly.

Skribble cleared his throat noisily and began, 'Well . . . um . . . perhaps I could accompany you a little way,' he mumbled. 'I mean, after all, such an event as this multiple-hatching is unique in the annals of creation. It should be documented by someone wise and objective, someone—'

'– who's cute as a button! Yippee!' shrieked Fenella. 'Oooh, Skribble, we'll have such fun, you and I. We'll have such adventures! See so many wondrous things. Oooh, you handsome little worm, you!' She popped a kiss on the top of Skribble's head.

He blushed furiously. 'Just be sure to educate your brood that I am not a mere earthworm! *I* am—'

'Perfect daddy material?' said Michael innocently.

Skribble stared at him, spluttering and speechless.

Milly looked at Jason and giggled.

'Come on, chicks!' said Fenella, throwing the rest of the worms hastily into her chicks' mouths. 'Time to go! Time to have your first proper flight!'

They all chirruped eagerly and gulped down the worms before flapping their wings and hopping to the edge of the workbench.

'Now, steady there, children,' said Skribble anxiously as the Milly-chick teetered on the edge. 'Just be careful! *Careful!*'

'Being careful only gets you so far.' Fenella turned to the children. 'Just remember, the future's wide open. Take a chance or two and you can be anything you want to be. Anything at all.'

Milly smiled and nodded. 'But do we really have to say goodbye?'

'Perhaps "Farewell" would be better.' She looked at each of them in turn, blue eyes sharp and sapphire-bright. 'Michael, Jess, Jason, Milly. Whenever I look at my precious chickabiddies' faces, I'll think of you.' A worried look crossed her face. 'But how will you remember me?'

'Oh, we'll remember you all right,' said Michael.

'No, no. I must give you something to remember me by. Something better than gold . . .' Fenella smiled suddenly. 'Wait a sec, loveys. I know just the thing!'

She plunged her curved beak into the feathers covering her chest and pulled out four, each with a shining jewel at its tip. 'Glow jewels,' she mumbled with her beak full of feathers. She flew around giving one feather with a jewel attached to each of them. 'From your tears,' she said, pressing the last feather into Milly's hands.

Milly looked at her in confusion.

'When you thought I was dead in that horrible room, lovey,' said Fenella, 'your tears fell on my heart. They helped revive me. And now it is my turn to give this gift to you. To all of you! Hold them close, and when you do, remember me and smile.' She looked around at them all, her blue eyes serious for once. 'My chicks wouldn't be here now if it wasn't for you. Thank you all.'

'Yes, thank you,' Skribble added. 'You are four fine children.' He regarded Michael and frowned. 'Well, three and a half, perhaps.'

'Oi!' Michael protested, and Fenella cast Skribble a sharp glance – but then they both caught the gleam in the magical bookworm's eye and smiled.

'It's been so lovely to see you again, Skribble,' Milly added, and Jess and Jason nodded.

'Next time, I hope the circumstances will be a little less frantic,' declared Skribble. 'Magic has bound us together, children, and such links can never be broken. Have no doubt of it – we shall meet again.'

Jess smiled. 'Maybe by then, I'll be a famous history expert!'

'And I'll be a rugby star!' Jason grinned.

'Me a famous actress,' said Milly in a grand diva voice.

Michael nodded. 'And I'll be a multi-multi-billionaire!'

Skribble glanced at Fenella and smiled. 'I dare say we are all of us richer for what's happened here.'

Fenella rose gracefully into the air. 'Now, time to fly, my little ones,' she trilled to her chicks. With excited cheeps the balls of fluff flapped their wings and rose unsteadily into the air. The golden bird tucked Skribble's lamp under one wing and winked at the children. 'Onwards to the great unknown!' she cried, and soared out through the door with the chicks following her, cheeping and turning somersaults as they went, and Skribble chivvying them on from behind.

'Bye-bye!' shouted Milly. 'I love you, Skribble! I love you, Fenella!'

'There they go,' Jason murmured, waving as the figures dwindled into the first golden stirrings of the sunset. 'The genie and the phoenix.'

'One of them lives for ever, the other one yabbers on for ever,' said Michael. He grinned. 'Good luck to them.'

'Wherever they fly,' said Milly dreamily.

'Now, we'd better get back home,' said Jess, 'and see about real life again.'

Together, chatting busily about all that had happened, Michael, Milly, Jason and Jess walked away from Mr Milton's place for the last time. The whole world around them seemed awake and alive with possibilities.

The children paused for a moment at the edge of the rambling grounds. Then, Michael pointed straight ahead and set off with a swagger in his step. 'Come on,' he said. 'The future's this way!'

ABOUT THE AUTHORS:

Steve Cole spent a happy childhood in rural Bedfordshire being loud and aspiring to amuse. He liked books and so went on to the university of East Anglia to read more of them. Later on he started writing them too, with titles ranging from pre-school poetry to young-adult thrillers (with more TV and film tie-ins than he cares to admit to along the way). In other careers, he has been the editor of *Noddy* magazine, and an editor of fiction and nonfiction book titles for various publishers.

Linda Chapman was born in 1969. Before becoming a full-time writer in 1999, she had many jobs, including being a teacher, stage manager, book-seller, university researcher and dog-trainer. She has written over seventy books for children, including the *My Secret Unicorn*, *Stardust* and *Not Quite a Mermaid* series. Linda lives in Leicestershire with her family and two Bernese Mountain dogs. When she is not writing she spends her time looking after her three young children, reading, putting on plays and horse riding.

GENIE US!
THE FIRST MAGICAL ADVENTURE FROM
BESTSELLING AUTHORS
STEVE COLE AND LINDA CHAPMAN

What would you wish for . . . ?

Take four ordinary children . . .
A genie in the shape of a bookworm . . .
And a magical book.

Then get ready for more adventure and mayhem then you
could ever imagine!

Join Michael, Milly, Jason and Jess as they dive into a world
of weirdness and wonder, trouble and trickery, trying to make
each other's wishes come true.

But when their wishes start to go wrong, the magic seems
scarier. If the children's greatest wish of all is finally
granted, will their world change for better or for worse?

ISBN: 978 1 862 30343 0

THE CITY OF EMBER
by Jeanne DuPrau

An underground city was built to save the human race.
It was to last 200 years . . .
Now, that time is up . . .

Food is low. Corruption is spreading. Worse of all, the lights
over the city are flickering. All that now stands between the
citizens of Ember and endless darkness are two teenagers
desperate to find a way out – before the lights go out for ever . . .

ESCAPE IS THE ONLY OPTION

'DuPrau is a most engaging writer'
TES

'An electric debut'
Publishers Weekly

ISBN: 978 0 552 55998 0

THE LONDON EYE MYSTERY
by Siobhan Dowd

What goes up, must come down . . . Mustn't it?

Monday 24 May, 11:32 a.m.
Ted and Kate watch their cousin Salim get on board the
London Eye. The pod rises from the ground.

Monday 24 May 12.02 p.m.
The pod lands and the doors open. People exit – but where is Salim?
When Aunty Gloria's son, Salim, mysteriously disappears from a
sealed pod on the London Eye, everyone is frantic.

Has he spontaneously combusted?
[Ted's theory.]

Has he been kidnapped?
[Aunt Gloria's theory]

Is he even still alive?
[The family's unspoken fear.]

Even the police are baffled. Ted, whose brain runs on its own
unique operating system, and his older sister, Kat, overcome their
prickly relationship to become sleuthing partners. They follow
a trail of clues across London in a desperate bid to find their
cousin, while time ticks dangerously by . . .

From the winner of the Branford Boase award

ISBN: 978 0 440 86802 6

TIM: DEFENDER OF THE EARTH
by Sam Enthoven

He's big, he's moody, he has a tail that could crush the Houses
of Parliament . . . and he's all that stands between the earth and
total destruction. (Oh, and he's actually pretty nice, razor-sharp
car-sized teeth notwithstanding.)

TIM (that's Tyrannosaurus Improved Model) is the product of a
top secret military experiment. He lives in a secret bunker under
Trafalgar Square – but now the government has decided he's too
expensive to keep and Tim must make a break for it.

He forms an unlikely alliance with fourteen year old Chris and
his classmate Anna in order to save humanity from the greatest
threat it has ever known:

Anna's father, the brilliant but demented Professor Mallahide
and his growing swarm of vicious nanobots.

The stage is set for a spectacular showdown the likes of
which London has never seen. Who will prevail? The
terrifying Professor Mallahide, or TIM, DEFENDER OF
THE EARTH . . . ?

ISBN: 978 0 385 60968 5